J.K. ROWLING

FANTASTIC BEASTS AND WHERE TO FIND THEM™

THE ORIGINAL SCREENPLAY

COVER AND BOOK DESIGN
BY
MINALIMA

sphere

SPHERE

First published in print in Great Britain in 2016 by Little, Brown

This paperback edition published in 2018 by Sphere

12

A CIP catalogue record for this book
is available from the British Library.

ISBN 978-0-7515-7495-1

Typeset in Crimson by MinaLima
Printed and bound in Great Britain by Clays Ltd, Elcograf S.p.A.

Papers used by Sphere are from well-managed forests
and other responsible sources.

Sphere
An imprint of
Little, Brown Book Group
Carmelite House
50 Victoria Embankment
London EC4Y 0DZ

An Hachette UK Company
www.hachette.co.uk

www.littlebrown.co.uk

FANTASTIC BEASTS AND WHERE TO FIND THEM™

THE ORIGINAL SCREENPLAY

To the memory of Gordon Murray,
real-life creature-healer and hero

CONTENTS

SCENE 1
EXT. SOMEWHERE IN EUROPE—1926—NIGHT

A large, isolated, derelict chateau emerges from the darkness. We focus on a cobbled square outside the building shrouded in mist, eerie, silent.

Five Aurors stand, wands aloft, tentative as they edge towards the chateau. A sudden explosion of pure white light sends them flying.

We whip round to find their bodies scattered, lying motionless at the entrance to a large parkland. A figure (GRINDELWALD) *enters the frame, his back to the camera; ignoring the bodies, he stares out into the night sky, as we pan up towards the moon.*

MONTAGE: we see various magical newspaper headlines from 1926 relating to GRINDELWALD'S *attacks all*

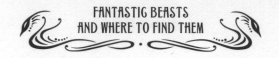

over the world – 'GRINDELWALD STRIKES AGAIN IN EUROPE', 'HOGWARTS SCHOOL INCREASES SECURITY', 'WHERE IS GRINDELWALD?'. He's a serious threat to the magical community and he's vanished. Moving photos detail destroyed buildings, fires, screaming victims. The articles come thick and fast – the worldwide hunt for GRINDELWALD *continues. We push in on a final article displaying the Statue of Liberty.*

TRANSITION TO:

SCENE 2
EXT. SHIP GLIDING INTO NEW YORK—NEXT MORNING

A bright, clear New York day. Seagulls swoop overhead.

A large passenger ship glides past the Statue of Liberty. Passengers lean over the rails, looking excitedly towards the oncoming land.

PUSH IN towards a figure sitting on a bench with his back to us – NEWT SCAMANDER, *weatherbeaten, wiry, wearing an old blue overcoat. Beside him rests a battered brown leather case. A catch on the case flicks open of its own accord.* NEWT *swiftly bends down to close it.*

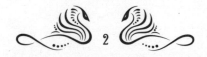

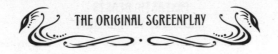

Placing the case on his lap, NEWT *leans in, whispering.*

NEWT
Dougal – you settle down
now, please. It won't be long.

SCENE 3
EXT. NEW YORK—DAY

AERIAL SHOT of New York.

SCENE 4
EXT. SHIP/INT. CUSTOMS—SHORTLY AFTERWARDS—DAY

Among bustling crowds, NEWT *walks down the gangplank of the ship, as we push in towards his case.*

CUSTOMS OFFICIAL (*O.S.*)
Next.

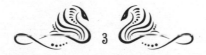

NEWT *stands at the Customs – a long row of desks by the shipyard, manned by serious-looking American officials. A* CUSTOMS OFFICIAL *examines* NEWT'S *very tattered British passport.*

CUSTOMS OFFICIAL
British, huh?

NEWT
Yes.

CUSTOMS OFFICIAL
First trip to New York?

NEWT
Yes.

CUSTOMS OFFICIAL
(gesturing to NEWT'S *case)*
Anything edible in there?

NEWT
(placing a hand over his breast pocket)
No.

CUSTOMS OFFICIAL
Livestock?

The catch on NEWT'S *case flicks open again.* NEWT *looks down and hastily closes it.*

NEWT
Must get that fixed – ah, no.

CUSTOMS OFFICIAL
(suspicious)
Let me take a look.

NEWT *places the case on the desk between them and discreetly flicks a brass dial to 'Muggleworthy'.*

The CUSTOMS OFFICIAL *spins the case towards him and pops the catches, lifting the lid to reveal pyjamas, various maps, a journal, an alarm clock, a magnifying glass and a Hufflepuff scarf. Finally satisfied, he closes the case.*

CUSTOMS OFFICIAL
Welcome to New York.

NEWT
Thank you.

NEWT *gathers his passport and case.*

CUSTOMS OFFICIAL
Next!

NEWT *exits through Customs.*

SCENE 5
EXT. STREET NEAR CITY HALL SUBWAY—DUSK

A long street of identical brownstone houses, one of which has been reduced to rubble. A gaggle of reporters and photographers mills around in the vague hope of something happening, but without much enthusiasm. One REPORTER *is interviewing an excitable middle-aged man as they move through the rubble.*

WITNESS
—and it was like a – like a *wind* or like a – like a *ghost* – but dark – and I saw its eyes – shinin' white eyes—

REPORTER
(expressionless – notebook in his hand)
—a dark wind – with eyes …

WITNESS
—like a dark *mass,* and it dove down there, down underground – I swear to God … into the earth right in front of me. Someone oughta do something about it. It's everywhere. It's outta control.

CLOSE ON PERCIVAL GRAVES *as he walks towards the destroyed building.*

GRAVES*: smart clothing, very handsome, early middle-age, his demeanour differs from those around him. He is watchful, tightly coiled, an air of intense confidence.*

PHOTOGRAPHER
(sotto voce)
Hey – did you get anything?

REPORTER
(sotto voce)
Dark wind, blah blah.

PHOTOGRAPHER
It's some atmospheric hooey. Or electrical.

GRAVES *moves up the steps of the now-ruined building. He examines the destruction, curious, alert.*

REPORTER
Hey – you thirsty?

PHOTOGRAPHER
Nah, I'm on the wagon.
Promised Martha I'd lay off.

The wind begins to pick up, swirling around the building, accompanied by a high-pitched screeching. GRAVES *alone looks interested.*

A sudden series of bangs at street level. All turn to look for the source of the sound: a wall cracks, the rubble on the floor begins to shake before exploding like an earthquake, ripping out of the building and down through the middle of the street. The movement is violent, rushed – people and cars go flying.

The mysterious force then flies up into the air, swirling through the city, diving in and out of alleyways, before crashing down into a subway station.

CLOSE ON GRAVES, *as he examines the destruction of the street.*

A mingled roar and howl emanates from the bowels of the earth.

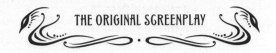

SCENE 6
EXT. NEW YORK STREET—DAY

Watching NEWT *walk, we see in him an unselfconscious Keatonesque quality, a sense of a different rhythm to those around him. In his hand he clutches directions on a small piece of paper, but he still shows a scientist's curiosity about this alien environment.*

SCENE 7
EXT. ANOTHER STREET, STEPS OF THE CITY BANK—DAY

NEWT, *intrigued by the noise of shouting, approaches a rally of the New Salem Philanthropic Society.*

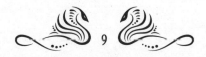

MARY LOU BAREBONE, *a handsome mid-western woman in a 1920s version of Puritan dress, charismatic and earnest, stands on a small stage at the steps to the City Bank. Behind her stands a man parading a banner emblazoned with the organisation's symbol: hands*

proudly grasping a broken wand amid bright yellow and red flames.

MARY LOU
(to the assembled crowd)
... this great city sparkles with the jewels of man's invention! Movie theatres, automobiles, the wireless, electric lights – all dazzle and bewitch us!

NEWT *slows down and watches* MARY LOU *as he would observe a foreign species: no judgement, simply interest. Nearby stands* TINA GOLDSTEIN, *hat low on her head, upturned collar. She is eating a hot dog, mustard smeared on her upper lip.* NEWT *accidently bumps into her as he makes his way to the front of the rally.*

NEWT
Oh ... so sorry.

MARY LOU
But where there is light there is shadow, friend. Something is stalking our city, wreaking destruction and then disappearing without a trace ...

JACOB KOWALSKI *moves nervously down the street towards the crowd, wearing an ill-fitting suit and carrying a battered brown leather case.*

MARY LOU (*O.S.*)
We have to fight – join us, the
Second Salemers, in our fight!

JACOB *makes his way through the gathered crowd, also pushing past* TINA.

JACOB
Excuse me doll, just trying to
get to the bank – excuse me –
just trying . . .

JACOB *trips over* NEWT'S *case, disappearing momentarily.* NEWT *hauls him up.*

NEWT
I'm so sorry – my case—

JACOB
No harm done—

JACOB *struggles on, heading past* MARY LOU *and up the steps of the bank.*

JACOB
Excuse me!

The kerfuffle around NEWT *draws* MARY LOU'S *attention.*

MARY LOU
(charming, to NEWT*)*
You, friend! What drew you
to our meeting today?

NEWT *is startled to find himself the centre of attention.*

NEWT
Oh . . . I was just . . . passing . . .

MARY LOU
Are you a seeker? A seeker
after truth?

A beat.

NEWT
I'm more of a chaser, really.

ANGLE ON people moving in and out of the bank.

A *smartly dressed man flips a dime towards a beggar sitting on the steps.*

CLOSE ON the dime, falling in slow motion.

MARY LOU (*O.S.*)
Hear my words and heed my warning . . .

ANGLE ON some little paws, which have appeared in the narrow crack between the lid and the body of NEWT'S *case.*

ANGLE ON the dime hitting the steps with a musical clang.

ANGLE ON the paws, now trying hard to prise open the case.

MARY LOU
. . . and laugh if you dare:
witches live among us!

MARY LOU'S *three adopted children, adults* CREDENCE *and* CHASTITY, *and* MODESTY *(an eight-year-old girl), hand out leaflets.* CREDENCE *appears nervous and troubled.*

MARY LOU (*O.S.*)
We have to fight together for the sake of our children – for the sake of tomorrow!
(*to* NEWT)
What do you say to that, friend?

As NEWT *looks up towards* MARY LOU, *something seen from the corner of his eye catches his attention. The Niffler, a small furry black cross between a mole and a duck-billed platypus, is sitting on the steps of the bank, hastily pulling the beggar's hat full of money out of sight behind a pillar.*

NEWT, *startled, looks down at his case.*

ANGLE ON the Niffler, busy shovelling the beggar's coins into a pouch in its belly. The Niffler looks up, notices NEWT'S *gaze, and hurriedly gathers the rest of the coins before tumbling away and into the bank.*

NEWT *jolts forwards.*

NEWT
Excuse me.

ANGLE ON MARY LOU *– she looks confused at* NEWT'S *lack of interest in her cause.*

MARY LOU (*O.S.*)
Witches live among us.

ANGLE ON TINA, *moving through the crowd, eyeing* NEWT *suspiciously.*

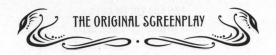

SCENE 8
INT. LOBBY OF BANK—MOMENTS LATER—DAY

A large, impressive-looking bank atrium. In the centre, behind a golden counter, clerks are busy at work serving customers.

NEWT *skids to a halt in the entrance of the space and looks around for his creature. His dress and demeanour make him out of place among the smartly dressed New Yorkers.*

BANK EMPLOYEE
(suspicious)
Can I help you, sir?

NEWT
No, I was just . . . just . . .
waiting . . .

NEWT *motions towards a bench and backs away, taking a seat next to* JACOB.

TINA *peers at* NEWT *from behind a pillar.*

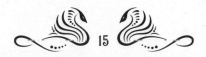

JACOB
(nervous)
Hi. What brings you here?

NEWT *is desperately trying to spot his Niffler.*

NEWT
Same as you . . .

JACOB
You're here to get a loan to open up a bakery?

NEWT
(looking around – preoccupied)
Yes.

JACOB
What are the odds of that? Well, may the best man win, I guess.

NEWT *spots the Niffler, which is now stealing coins from someone's bag.*

JACOB *holds out his hand, but* NEWT *is off.*

NEWT
Excuse me.

NEWT *darts away. In his place on the bench lies a large silver egg.*

JACOB
Hey, mister ... hey mister!

NEWT *doesn't hear; he is too engaged in hunting the Niffler.*

JACOB *picks up the egg just as the door into the* BANK MANAGER'S *office opens, and a* SECRETARY *looks out.*

JACOB
Hey, fella!

SECRETARY
Mr Kowalski, Mr Bingley will see you now.

Pocketing the egg, JACOB *heads towards the office, steeling himself.*

JACOB
(sotto voce)
Okay ... okay.

ANGLE ON NEWT, *surreptitiously pursuing the Niffler as it moves through the bank. He finally spots it removing a glittering buckle from a lady's shoe before scurrying onwards, eager for more shiny objects.*

As NEWT *watches, helpless, the Niffler jumps lithely between cases and into bags, snatching and pilfering.*

SCENE 9

INT. BINGLEY'S OFFICE—MOMENTS LATER—DAY

JACOB *is facing the imposing and impeccably suited* MR BINGLEY. BINGLEY *is examining* JACOB'S *business proposal for a bakery.*

An uncomfortable silence. The sound of a ticking clock and BINGLEY *murmuring.*

JACOB *looks down at his pocket – the egg has started to vibrate.*

BINGLEY
You are currently working …
in a canning factory?

JACOB
That's the best I can do – I
only got back in '24.

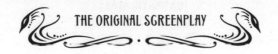

BINGLEY
Got back?

JACOB
From Europe, sir. Yeah – I was part of the Expeditionary Forces there—

JACOB *is clearly nervous, miming a digging action to the words 'Expeditionary Forces', in the vain hope that a joke might help his cause.*

SCENE 10
INT. BACK ROOM OF THE BANK—MOMENTS LATER—DAY

We cut back to NEWT *in the bank – in seeking the Niffler he has ended up waiting in line for a bank teller. He cranes his neck, peering towards the bag of a lady at the front of the line.* TINA *watches him from behind a pillar.*

ANGLE ON coins spilling from underneath a bench.

ANGLE ON NEWT, *who hears the coins and turns to see small paws hastily gathering them up.*

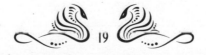

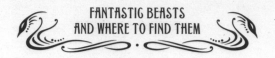

ANGLE ON the Niffler sitting under the bench looking fat and smug. Not yet satisfied, its attention is caught by the shiny tag hanging around the neck of a small dog. The Niffler moves slowly, cheekily, forwards – little paw outstretched to grab the tag. The dog snarls and barks.

NEWT *starts forwards and dives under the bench – the Niffler runs, scuttling over the bank counter screens and out of* NEWT'S *reach.*

SCENE 11
INT. BINGLEY'S OFFICE—MOMENTS LATER—DAY

JACOB *opens his case with great pride. Inside is displayed a selection of his home-made pastries.*

JACOB (*O.S.*)
All right.

BINGLEY
Mr Kowalski—

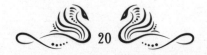

JACOB
—you gotta try the paczki okay, it's my grandmother's recipe, the orange zest – just—

JACOB *holds out a paczki . . .* BINGLEY *is not distracted.*

BINGLEY
Mr Kowalski, what do you propose to offer the bank as collateral?

JACOB
Collateral?

BINGLEY
Collateral.

JACOB *gestures hopefully towards his pastries.*

BINGLEY
There are machines now that can produce hundreds of doughnuts an hour—

JACOB
I know, I know, but they're nothing like what I can do—

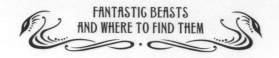

BINGLEY
The bank must be protected, Mr Kowalski. Good day to you.

BINGLEY *dismissively rings a bell on his desk.*

SCENE 12
INT. BEHIND THE BANK COUNTERS—MOMENTS LATER—DAY

The Niffler sits on a trolley covered in money bags, which it greedily empties into its pouch. As NEWT *watches through the security bars, aghast, a guard pushes the trolley away down a corridor.*

SCENE 13
INT. BANK, HALL—MOMENTS LATER—DAY

JACOB, *downcast, exits* BINGLEY'S *office. His bulging*

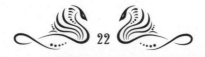

pocket vibrates. Alarmed, he pulls out the egg and looks around.

ANGLE ON the Niffler, still sitting on the trolley, which is now being pushed into an elevator.

ANGLE ON JACOB, *who sees* NEWT *in the distance.*

JACOB
Hey, Mr English guy! I think your egg is hatching.

NEWT *looks hurriedly between* JACOB *and the shutting elevator doors before making a decision: he points his wand at* JACOB. JACOB *and the egg are pulled magically across the bank atrium towards* NEWT. *In a split second, they Disapparate.*

TINA *stares, incredulous, from behind a pillar.*

SCENE 14
INT. BACK ROOM OF THE BANK/STAIRCASE—DAY

NEWT *and* JACOB *Apparate into a narrow stairwell*

leading to the bank's vaults, suddenly past the tellers and security guards.

NEWT *gently takes the egg back from* JACOB *as it hatches, revealing a small blue, snake-like bird – an Occamy.* NEWT, *his face full of wonder, looks to* JACOB *as though expecting a similar reaction from him.*

Slowly, NEWT *carries the baby creature down the stairs.*

JACOB
Excuse me . . .

JACOB, *very confused, looks back up the stairs towards the main bank atrium. On seeing* BINGLEY *approaching, he ducks down the stairs, out of sight.*

JACOB
(to himself)
I was – over there. I was –
over there?

<u>SCENE 15</u>
INT. BASEMENT CORRIDOR OF BANK LEADING TO VAULT—DAY

JACOB'S *POV:* NEWT *is crouched down, opening his case. He carefully places the hatched Occamy inside, whispering tenderly:*

NEWT
In you hop . . .

JACOB (*O.S.*)
Hello?

NEWT
No. Everyone settle down – stay. Dougal, don't make me come in there . . .

JACOB *moves along the corridor, staring at* NEWT.

We see a strange green creature, part stick insect, part plant, poke its head out of NEWT'S *breast pocket, intrigued. This is* PICKETT, *a Bowtruckle.*

NEWT
Don't make me come down there.

NEWT *looks up to see the Niffler squeezing itself through locked doors, into the central vault.*

NEWT
Absolutely not!

NEWT *takes out his wand and points it at the vault.*

NEWT
Alohomora.

We watch the locks and cogs of the vault door turn.

BINGLEY *comes round the corner, just as the vault door starts to open.*

BINGLEY
(*to* JACOB)
Oh, so you're gonna STEAL
the money, huh?

BINGLEY *hits a button on the wall. An alarm sounds.* NEWT *aims his wand . . .*

NEWT
Petrificus Totalus.

BINGLEY *suddenly stiffens and falls back flat on the ground.* JACOB *cannot believe his eyes.*

JACOB

Mr Bingley!

The vault door opens wide.

MR BINGLEY

(in his paralysed state)

... Kowalski!

NEWT *hurries into the vault. Inside he finds the Niffler lying among hundreds of opened deposit boxes, and seated on a great pile of cash. The Niffler stares at* NEWT *defiantly as it forces another gold bar into its already overflowing pouch.*

NEWT

Really?!

NEWT *grasps the Niffler tightly and turns it upside down, shaking it by its hind legs. An extraordinary, and seemingly endless, number of precious items fall out.*

NEWT

(to the Niffler)

No ...

JACOB *looks around him in disbelief, an almost queasy fear.*

Despite their altercation, NEWT *is fond of the Niffler. He grins as he tickles its stomach, causing more treasure to pour out.*

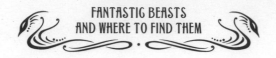

Footsteps on the stairs as several armed guards run down and into the vault corridor.

JACOB
(panicking)
Oh no . . . no . . . don't shoot.
Don't shoot!

NEWT *quickly seizes* JACOB *and the two of them, plus the Niffler and case, Disapparate.*

<u>SCENE 16</u>
EXT. DESERTED SIDE STREET NEXT TO THE BANK—DAY

NEWT *and* JACOB *Apparate into a side street. Security alarms ring out from the bank and, at the end of the side street, we see crowds gathering, police arriving.*

TINA *runs out of the bank and looks down. She sees* NEWT *wrestling the Niffler back into the case,* JACOB *cowering by a wall.*

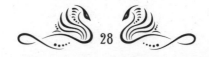

JACOB
Ahhh!

NEWT
For the last time, you pilfering pest – paws off what doesn't belong to you!

NEWT *shuts his case, then looks around at* JACOB.

NEWT
I'm awfully sorry about all that—

JACOB
What the *hell* was that?

NEWT
Nothing that need concern you. Now unfortunately you have seen far too much, so if you wouldn't mind – if you just stand there – this will be over in a jiffy.

NEWT, *trying to find his wand, turns his back on* JACOB. JACOB *takes the opportunity, seizes his case, and swings it violently at* NEWT, *who is knocked to the ground.*

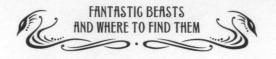

JACOB

Sorry—

JACOB *runs for his life.*

NEWT *holds his head for a moment and looks after* JACOB, *who has hurried down the alleyway and into the crowd.*

NEWT

Bugger!

TINA *comes walking down the side street with purpose.* NEWT *gathers himself, picks up the case and, trying to be nonchalant, walks towards her. As he passes her,* TINA *grabs* NEWT'S *elbow and they Disapparate.*

<u>SCENE 17</u>
EXT. NARROW ALLEYWAY OPPOSITE BANK—DAY

NEWT *and* TINA *Apparate into a cramped, bricked-up alleyway. We can still hear police sirens sounding in the background.*

TINA, *incredulous and out of breath, rounds on* NEWT.

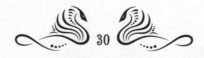

TINA

Who *are* you?

NEWT

I'm sorry?

TINA

Who *are you?*

NEWT

Newt Scamander. And you are?

TINA

What's that *thing* in your case?

NEWT

That's my Niffler.

(pointing at hot dog mustard still on TINA'S *lip)*

Er, you've got something on your—

TINA

Why in the name of Deliverance Dane did you let that thing loose?

NEWT
I didn't mean to – he's incorrigible, you see, anything shiny, he's all over the place—

TINA
You didn't mean to?

NEWT
No.

TINA
You could not have chosen a worse time to let that creature loose! We're in the middle of a situation here! I'm taking you in.

NEWT
You're taking me where?

She produces her official ID card. It bears her moving picture and an impressive symbol of an American eagle: MACUSA.

TINA
Magical Congress of the United States of America.

NEWT
(nervous)
So, you work for MACUSA? What are you, some kind of investigator?

TINA
(hesitates)
Uh huh.

She stuffs her identification card back into her coat.

TINA
Can you please tell me you took care of the No-Maj?

NEWT
The what?

TINA
(becoming irritated)
The No-Maj! No-magic – the non-wizard!

NEWT
Oh sorry, we call them Muggles.

TINA

(getting really worried)

You wiped his memory, right? The No-Maj with the case?

NEWT

Um …

TINA

(appalled)

That's a Section 3A, Mr Scamander. I'm taking you in.

She takes NEWT *by the arm and they Disapparate again.*

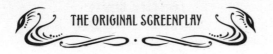

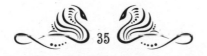

<u>SCENE 18</u>
EXT. BROADWAY—DAY

An ornately carved, incredibly tall skyscraper on the corner of a bustling street – the Woolworth Building.

NEWT *and* TINA *hurry along Broadway towards this building,* TINA *almost dragging* NEWT *by his coat sleeve.*

TINA
Come on.

NEWT
Er – sorry but I do have
things to do, actually.

TINA
Well, you'll have to rearrange them!

TINA *forcefully guides* NEWT *through the busy traffic.*

TINA
What are you doing in New York anyway?

NEWT
I came to buy a birthday present.

TINA
Couldn't you have done that in London?

They have arrived outside the Woolworth Building. Workers move in and out of a large revolving door.

NEWT
No, there's only one breeder of Appaloosa Puffskeins in the world and he lives in New York, so no ...

TINA *moves* NEWT *towards a side door, guarded by a man in a cloaked uniform.*

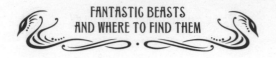

TINA
(to the guard)
I got a Section 3A.

The guard immediately opens the door.

SCENE 19
INT. WOOLWORTH BUILDING RECEPTION—DAY

A normal 1920s office atrium, people milling around and chatting.

TINA *(O.S.)*
Hey. We don't allow the breeding of magical creatures in New York. We closed that guy down a year ago, by the way.

PAN AROUND to watch TINA *come through the door with* NEWT*. As they enter, the whole entrance magically transforms from the Woolworth Building to the Magical Congress of the United States of America (MACUSA).*

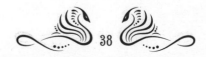

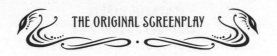

SCENE 20
INT. MACUSA LOBBY—DAY

NEWT'S *POV, as they move up a wide staircase and enter the main lobby – a vast, impressive space with impossibly high vaulted ceilings.*

High up, a gigantic dial with many cogs and faces emblazoned with the legend: MAGICAL EXPOSURE THREAT LEVEL. The hand on the dial points to SEVERE: UNEXPLAINED ACTIVITY. Behind hangs an imposing portrait of a majestic-looking witch: SERAPHINA PICQUERY, *MACUSA's President.*

Owls circulate, witches and wizards in 1920s dress are hard at work. TINA *guides an impressed-looking* NEWT *through the bustle. They pass several wizards sitting in a line, waiting to have their wands shined by a house-elf who operates a complex contraption of feathers.*

NEWT *and* TINA *reach an elevator. The doors open to reveal* RED, *a goblin bellboy.*

RED
Hey, Goldstein.

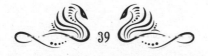

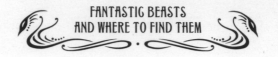

TINA
Hey, Red.

TINA *pushes* NEWT *inside.*

<u>SCENE 21</u>
INT. ELEVATOR—DAY

TINA
(*to* RED)
Major Investigation Department.

RED
I thought you was—

TINA
Major Investigation Department! I got a Section 3A!

RED *uses a long clawed stick to reach an elevator button above his head. The elevator descends.*

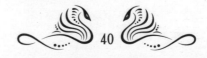

SCENE 22
INT. MAJOR INVESTIGATION DEPARTMENT—DAY

CLOSE ON a newspaper – The New York Ghost – *with the headline 'MAGICAL DISTURBANCES RISK WIZARDING EXPOSURE'.*

A group of the highest-level Aurors in the organisation are gathered together in serious discussion. Among them are GRAVES, *examining the newspaper, his face cut and bruised from last night's encounter with the strange entity, and* MADAM PICQUERY *herself.*

MADAM PICQUERY
The International Confederation is threatening to send a delegation. They think this is related to Grindelwald's attacks in Europe.

GRAVES
I was there. This is a beast. No human could do what this

thing is capable of, Madam President.

MADAM PICQUERY (*O.S.*)
Whatever it is, one thing's clear – it must be stopped. It's terrorising No-Majs, and when No-Majs are afraid, they attack. This could mean exposure. It could mean war.

On hearing footsteps, the group looks round to see TINA, *who approaches cautiously, leading* NEWT.

MADAM PICQUERY
(angry but contained)
I made your position here quite clear, Miss Goldstein.

TINA
(frightened)
Yes, Madam President, but I—

MADAM PICQUERY
You are no longer an Auror.

TINA
No, Madam President, but—

MADAM PICQUERY
Goldstein.

TINA
There's been a minor incident—

MADAM PICQUERY
Well, this office is currently concerned with very major incidents. Get out.

TINA
(humiliated)
Yes, ma'am.

TINA *pushes a bemused-looking* NEWT *back towards the elevator.* GRAVES *looks after them, the only one to appear sympathetic.*

SCENE 23
INT. BASEMENT—DAY

The elevator descends rapidly through the long shaft.

The doors open onto a cramped, airless, windowless basement room. A painful contrast to the floor above. Clearly the place where utter no-hopers work.

TINA *leads* NEWT *past a hundred typewriters clacking away unmanned, with a tangle of glass pipes hanging down from the ceiling above them.*

As each memo or form is completed by a typewriter, it folds itself into an origami rat, which scurries up the appropriate tube to the offices above. Two rats collide and fight, tearing each other apart.

TINA *walks towards a dingy corner of the room. A sign: WAND PERMIT OFFICE.*

NEWT *ducks under it.*

<u>SCENE 24</u>
INT. WAND PERMIT OFFICE—DAY

The Wand Permit Office is only slightly larger than a cupboard. There are piles of unopened wand applications.

TINA *stops behind a desk, removing her coat and hat. She tries to regain her lost status in front of* NEWT *by appearing official, busying herself with papers.*

TINA
So, you got your wand permit? All foreigners have to have them in New York.

NEWT
(lying)
I made a postal application weeks ago.

TINA
(now sitting on the desk, scribbles on a clipboard)
Scamander …
(finding him very fishy)
And you were just in Equatorial Guinea?

NEWT
I've just completed a year in the field. I'm writing a book about magical creatures.

TINA
Like – an extermination guide?

NEWT
No. A guide to help people understand why we should be protecting these creatures instead of killing them.

ABERNATHY (*O.S.*)
GOLDSTEIN! Where is she? Where is she? GOLDSTEIN!

TINA *ducks behind her desk, which amuses* NEWT.

ABERNATHY, *a pompous jobsworth, enters. He immediately realises where* TINA *is hidden.*

ABERNATHY
Goldstein!

TINA, *looking guilty, slowly emerges from behind the desk.*

ABERNATHY
Did you just butt in on the Investigative Team again?

TINA *is about to defend herself, but* ABERNATHY *continues.*

ABERNATHY
Where've you been?

TINA
(awkward)
What . . .?

ABERNATHY
(to NEWT*)*
Where'd she pick you up?

NEWT
Me?

NEWT *quickly looks at* TINA, *who shakes her head, her expression one of desperation.* NEWT *stalls – a silent pact between him and* TINA.

ABERNATHY
(agitated by the lack of information)
Have you been tracking them Second Salemers again?

TINA
Of course not, sir.

GRAVES *comes round the corner.* ABERNATHY *is immediately cowed.*

ABERNATHY
Afternoon, Mr Graves, sir!

GRAVES

Afternoon, ah – Abernathy.

TINA *steps forwards to formally address* GRAVES.

TINA

(speaking quickly, eager to have her case heard)

Mr Graves, sir, this is Mr Scamander – he has a crazy creature in that case and it got out and caused mayhem in a bank.

GRAVES

Let's see the little guy.

TINA *breathes a sigh of relief: finally someone is listening to her.* NEWT *tries to speak up – he looks more panicky than might seem warranted by a Niffler – but* GRAVES *dismisses him.*

TINA *theatrically places the case onto a table and throws open the lid. She looks aghast at the contents.*

ANGLE ON the case contents – it is full of pastries. NEWT *approaches, nervous. On seeing the contents he looks horrified.* GRAVES *looks confused, but smirks slightly – another one of* TINA'S *mistakes.*

GRAVES

Tina . . .

GRAVES *walks away.* NEWT *and* TINA *stare at each other.*

SCENE 25
EXT. STREET ON THE LOWER EAST SIDE—DAY

JACOB *marches along the overcast street, case in hand, past pushcarts, shabby little shops and tenement buildings. He continually throws nervous glances over his shoulder.*

SCENE 26
INT. JACOB'S ROOM—DAY

A tiny, dirty room, the furnishings sparse and shabby.

CLOSE ON the case as JACOB *throws it down onto his bed. He looks up at a portrait of his grandmother, which hangs on the wall.*

JACOB
I'm sorry, Grandma.

JACOB *sits down at his desk, hanging his head in his hands, downcast, tired. Behind him, one of the catches on the case flies open.* JACOB *turns ...*

He sits down on the bed and examines the case. The second catch now flicks open of its own accord, and the case begins to shake, emitting aggressive animalistic sounds. JACOB *slowly backs away.*

Tentatively, he leans forward ... suddenly the lid flies open and out bursts a Murtlap – a rat-like creature with an anemone-style growth on its back. JACOB *grapples with it, holding it tightly in both hands as it struggles.*

We whip back to the case, which flies open once again as an invisible being shoots out, crashing into the ceiling before smashing through the window.

The Murtlap lunges forwards, biting JACOB *on the neck, sending him crashing through furniture and tumbling to the ground.*

The room shakes heavily, and the wall holding the picture of JACOB'S *grandma begins to crack before exploding, as more creatures escape off-screen.*

SCENE 27
INT. SECOND SALEM CHURCH, MAIN HALL—DAY—MONTAGE

A dingy wooden church with darkened windows and a high mezzanine balcony. MODESTY *is playing a solitary variation of hopscotch, skipping in and out of a chalked grid.*

MODESTY
My momma, your momma,
gonna catch a witch
My momma, your momma,
flying on a switch
My momma, your momma,
witches never cry

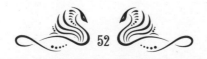

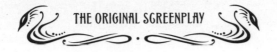

My momma, your momma,
witches gonna die!

As she sings we see the church is full of group paraphernalia – leaflets advertising MARY LOU'S *campaign, and a large version of the group's anti-witchcraft banner.*

SCENE 28
INT. SECOND SALEM CHURCH, MAIN HALL—DAY

A pigeon coos from a high-up window. CREDENCE *steps forwards, staring up towards it before mechanically clapping his hands. The pigeon flies away.*

We follow CHASTITY *as she moves through the church and opens the large double doors onto the street.*

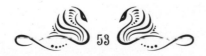

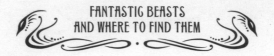

<u>SCENE 29</u>
EXT. SECOND SALEM CHURCH, BACKYARD—DAY

CHASTITY *emerges from the church and rings a large dinner bell.*

<u>SCENE 30</u>
INT. SECOND SALEM CHURCH, MAIN HALL—DAY

MODESTY *continues playing hopscotch.* CREDENCE *pauses, looking past her and out towards the door.*

MODESTY
Witch number three, gonna
watch her burn,
Witch number four, flogging
take a turn.

Young children stream into the church.

TIME CUT:

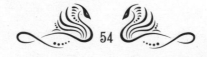

Brown soup is being ladled out to the children, who jostle each other to get near the front of the line. MARY LOU, *wearing an apron and looking on approvingly, squeezes through the little crowd.*

MARY LOU
Collect your leaflets before
you get food, children.

Several of the children turn towards CHASTITY, *who waits primly, handing out campaign leaflets.*

TIME CUT:

MARY LOU *and* CREDENCE *ladle out soup,* CREDENCE *looking intently into every face.*

A BOY *with a birthmark on his face reaches the front of the line.* CREDENCE *stops his work and stares at him.* MARY LOU *reaches out to touch the* BOY'S *face.*

BOY
Is it a witch's mark, ma'am?

MARY LOU
No. He's okay.

The BOY *takes his soup and leaves.* CREDENCE *stares after him, as they continue to serve.*

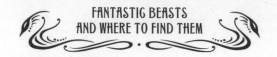

SCENE 31
EXT. MAIN STREET ON THE LOWER EAST SIDE—AFTERNOON

CLOSE ON a Billywig – a small blue creature with helicopter-like wings on its head – flying high above the street.

TINA *and* NEWT *walk along the street,* TINA *carrying the case.*

TINA
(on the verge of tears)
I can't *believe* you didn't Obliviate that man! If there's an inquiry I'm finished!

NEWT
So why would you be finished? I'm the one that's—

TINA
I'm not supposed to go near the Second Salemers!

The Billywig zooms over their heads. NEWT *spins, horrified, watching it.*

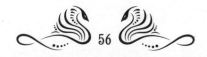

TINA
What was that?

NEWT
Er – moth, I think. Big moth.

TINA *finds this explanation dubious. They round a corner to find a crowd gathered in front of a crumbling building. People are shouting, others are hurriedly evacuating the building. A* POLICEMAN *is standing at the centre of the crowd, being harassed by disgruntled tenement-dwellers.*

JUMP CUT:

NEWT *and* TINA *move around the outskirts of the crowd. At the back, a tipsy* HOBO *is trying to attract the* POLICEMAN'S *attention.*

POLICEMAN
Hey . . . hey – quiet down – I'm trying to get a statement . . .

HOUSEWIFE
. . . I'm telling you it's a gas explosion again, I ain't taking the kids back up there until it's safe.

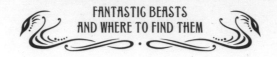

POLICEMAN
Sorry, ma'am – there ain't no smell of gas.

HOBO
(drunk)
It warn't gas – hey, officer, I seen it! – it wuzza – a gigantic – a huge hippopotto—

TINA *is looking up at the ruined building, and misses* NEWT *sliding his wand from his sleeve and pointing it at the* HOBO.

HOBO
—gas. It was gas.

The others in the crowd around him agree.

CROWD
Gas . . . it was gas!

TINA *again catches sight of the Billywig. Taking advantage of this distraction,* NEWT *runs up the metal steps and inside the ruined tenement building.*

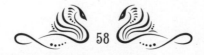

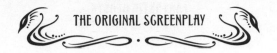

SCENE 32
INT. JACOB'S ROOM—AFTERNOON

NEWT *enters* JACOB'S *room and stops, staring: the room is completely destroyed. Footprints, broken furniture, shattered glass. Even worse: a massive hole in the opposite wall – something huge has blasted its way out. We can hear* JACOB *groaning from the corner.*

SCENE 33
EXT. TENEMENT STREET—AFTERNOON

CUT BACK TO TINA *as she looks around and realises that* NEWT *has disappeared from the crowd.*

SCENE 34
INT. JACOB'S ROOM

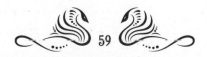

NEWT *crouches beside* JACOB, *who lies on his back, eyes closed and moaning.* NEWT *tries to examine a small red*

bite on JACOB'S *neck, but* JACOB *keeps unconsciously batting him away.*

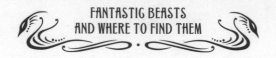

TINA (*O.S.*)
Mr Scamander!

CUT TO TINA, *running with purpose up the staircase of* JACOB'S *building.*

CUT BACK TO NEWT, *who desperately performs a repairing charm. The room is righted, the wall repaired, just in time before* TINA *enters the room.*

<u>SCENE 35</u>

INT. JACOB'S ROOM—AFTERNOON

TINA *hurries inside to find* NEWT, *trying to look innocent and composed, sitting on the bed. He calmly seals the latches on his case.*

TINA
It was *open*?

NEWT
Just a smidge . . .

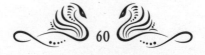

TINA
That crazy Niffler thing's on the loose again?

NEWT
Er – it *might* be—

TINA
Then look for it! Look!

JACOB *moans.*

TINA *drops* JACOB'S *case and makes straight for the injured* JACOB.

TINA
(*worried about* JACOB)
His neck's bleeding, he's hurt! Wake up, Mr No-Maj . . .

With TINA'S *back turned,* NEWT *makes towards the door. Suddenly,* TINA *emits a guttural scream as the Murtlap comes scuttling out from under a cabinet and latches onto her arm.* NEWT *spins, catching the creature by the tail and grappling it into the case.*

TINA
Mercy Lewis, what is that?

NEWT

Nothing to worry about. That is a Murtlap.

Unnoticed by either, JACOB *opens his eyes.*

TINA

What else have you got in there?

JACOB

(recognising NEWT*)*

You!

NEWT

Hello.

TINA

Easy, Mr—

JACOB

Kowalski . . . Jacob . . .

TINA *takes* JACOB'S *hand to shake it.*

NEWT *raises his wand.* JACOB *recoils in fear, clutching at* TINA, *who moves protectively in front of him.*

TINA
You can't Obliviate him! We need him as a witness.

NEWT
I'm sorry – you've just yelled at me the length of New York for not doing it in the first place . . .

TINA
He's hurt! He looks ill!

NEWT
He'll be fine. Murtlap bites aren't serious.

NEWT *puts his wand away.* JACOB *retches into the corner, while* TINA *looks at* NEWT *in disbelief.*

NEWT
I admit that is a slightly more severe reaction than I've seen, but if it was really serious – he'd have . . .

TINA
What?

NEWT

Well, the first symptom would be flames out of his anus—

TINA

This is balled up!

NEWT

It'll last forty-eight hours at most! I can keep him if you want me to—

TINA

Oh, keep him? We don't keep them! Mr Scamander, do you know *anything* about the wizarding community in America?

NEWT

I do know a few things, actually. I know you have rather backwards laws about relations with non-magic people. That you're not meant to befriend them, that you can't marry them, which seems mildly absurd to me.

JACOB *is following this conversation, open-mouthed.*

TINA
Who's going to marry him? You're both coming with me—

NEWT
I don't see why I need to come with you—

TINA *tries to lift the partially conscious* JACOB *from the floor.*

TINA
Help me!

NEWT *feels obliged to help.*

JACOB
I'm . . . I'm dreaming, right? Yeah . . . I'm tired, I never went to the bank. This is all just some big nightmare, right?

TINA
For the both of us, Mr Kowalski.

TINA *and* NEWT *Disapparate with* JACOB.

We focus on the photo of JACOB'S *grandma, once again hanging on the wall. Eventually the photo gives a little shake before falling and revealing a hole in the wall, inhabited by the Niffler.*

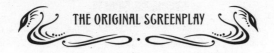

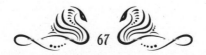

SCENE 36
EXT. UPPER EAST SIDE—AFTERNOON

A young boy, clutching a huge lollipop, is led down the busy street by his father. As they pass a fruit barrow, an apple suddenly levitates, bobbing along beside him. The boy gazes in wonder as the apple is eaten by something invisible, then the smile fades as his lollipop is snatched by the same unseen hands.

At a newsstand, the eyes of a lady on an advertisement blink open. The outline of a creature becomes visible, camouflage-like, before it peels away from the poster. It moves along the street, invisible again, only locatable by the lollipop it holds – seemingly suspended in mid-air. A dog

barks in its direction, and the creature scuttles on, knocking over newspaper stands, causing bikes and cars to swerve.

ANGLE ON the roof of a department store – we see a thin blue tail slither inside a small attic window. Suddenly the building shakes and tiles break away, as the creature's size expands to fill the whole room.

<u>SCENE 37</u>
INT. SHAW TOWER NEWSROOM—DUSK

The glittering Art Deco headquarters of a media empire. Many journalists are hard at work in an outer office.

An elevator opens and LANGDON SHAW *bustles excitedly through the room, leading the Second Salemers. He carries maps, several old books and a handful of photographs.*

MARY LOU *is composed,* CHASTITY *looks shy and* MODESTY *is excited, curious.* CREDENCE *looks nervous – he doesn't like crowds.*

LANGDON
. . . and so this is the newsroom.

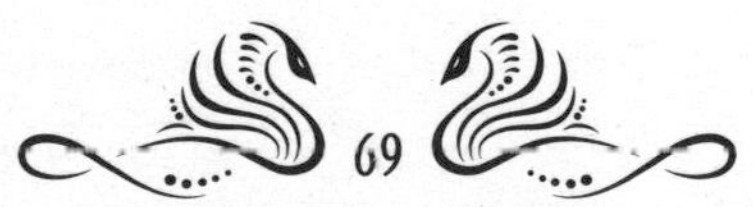

LANGDON *spins around excitedly, eager to show the Second Salemers that he holds authority here.*

LANGDON
Let's go!

LANGDON *moves around the office and speaks to some of the workers.*

LANGDON
Hey, how are you? Make way for the Barebones! Now, they're just putting the papers to bed, as they say.

Looks of veiled amusement from journalists as LANGDON *leads his group to double doors at the end of the open-plan area.* HENRY SHAW SR'S *assistant* – BARKER – *stands up, anxious.*

BARKER
Mr Shaw, sir, he's with the senator—

LANGDON
Never mind that, Barker, I wanna see my father!

LANGDON *pushes past.*

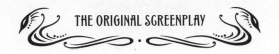

SCENE 38
INT. SHAW SR'S PENTHOUSE OFFICE—DUSK

A large, impressive office with spectacular views across the city. The newspaper magnate – HENRY SHAW SR *– is talking to his elder son,* SENATOR SHAW.

SENATOR SHAW
... we could just buy the boats ...

The doors burst open to reveal a harassed-looking BARKER *and an excitable* LANGDON.

BARKER
I'm so sorry, Mr Shaw, but your son insisted—

LANGDON
Father, you're going to want to hear this.

LANGDON *moves towards his father's desk and begins spreading out photographs. We recognise some of the images: the destroyed streets from the start of the film.*

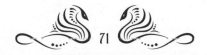

LANGDON
I've got something huge!

SHAW SR
Your brother and I are busy here, Langdon. Working on his election campaign. We don't have time for this.

MARY LOU, CREDENCE, CHASTITY *and* MODESTY *enter the office.* SHAW SR *and* SENATOR SHAW *stare.* CREDENCE *stands with his head bowed, embarrassed, nervous.*

LANGDON
This is Mary Lou Barebone from the New Salem Philanthropic Society, and she's got a big story for you!

SHAW SR
Oh she has – has she?

LANGDON
There's strange things going on all over the city. The people behind this – they are not like you and me. This is witchcraft, don't you see?

SHAW SR *and the* SENATOR *look dubious – all too used to* LANGDON'S *harebrained little projects and interests.*

SHAW SR

Langdon.

LANGDON

She doesn't want any money.

SHAW SR

Then either her story is worthless, or she's lying about the cost. Nobody gives away anything valuable for free.

MARY LOU

(confident, persuasive)

You are right, Mr Shaw. What we desire is infinitely more valuable than money: it's your influence. Millions of people read your newspapers and they need to be made aware about this danger.

LANGDON

The crazy disturbances in the subway – just look at the pictures!

SHAW SR

I'd like you and your friends to leave.

LANGDON

No, you're missing a trick here. Just look at the evidence—

SHAW SR

Really.

SENATOR SHAW

(joining his father and brother)

Langdon. Listen to Father and just go.

His eyes shift, focus on CREDENCE.

SENATOR SHAW

And take the freaks with you.

CREDENCE *perceptibly twitches, disturbed by anger in his vicinity.* MARY LOU *is calm, but steely.*

LANGDON

This is Father's office, not yours, and I'm sick of this every time I walk in here . . .

SHAW SR *silences his son and motions for the* BAREBONES *to leave.*

SHAW SR
That's it – thank you.

MARY LOU
(calm, dignified)
We hope you'll reconsider, Mr Shaw. We're not difficult to find. Until then, we thank you for your time.

SHAW SR *and* SENATOR SHAW *watch* MARY LOU *as she turns, leading her children out. The newsroom has fallen quiet, everyone craning to hear the row.*

As he departs, CREDENCE *drops a leaflet.* SENATOR SHAW *moves forwards and bends to pick it up. He glances at the witches on the front.*

SENATOR SHAW
(to CREDENCE*)*
Hey, boy. You dropped something.

The SENATOR *crumples up the leaflet before putting it in* CREDENCE'S *hand.*

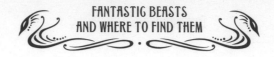

SENATOR SHAW
Here you go, freak – why don't you put that in the trash where you all belong.

Behind CREDENCE, MODESTY'S *eyes burn. She clutches* CREDENCE'S *hand protectively.*

SCENE 39
EXT. BROWNSTONE STREET—SHORTLY AFTERWARDS—DUSK

TINA *and* NEWT *stand on either side of an ailing* JACOB, *trying to keep him steady.*

TINA
Take a right here . . .

JACOB *makes various retching sounds, the bite on his neck clearly affecting him more and more.*

As the group rounds a corner, TINA *hurries them to hide behind a large repair truck. From here she peers at a house across the street.*

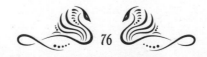

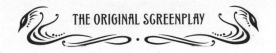

TINA

Okay – before we go in – I'm not supposed to have men on the premises.

NEWT

In that case, Mr Kowalski and I can easily seek other accommodation—

TINA

Oh no, you don't!

TINA *quickly grabs* JACOB'S *arm and pulls him across the road,* NEWT *dutifully following.*

TINA

Watch your step.

<u>SCENE 40</u>

INT. GOLDSTEIN RESIDENCE, STAIRWELL—DUSK

NEWT, TINA *and* JACOB *tiptoe up the stairs. They have just reached the first landing when* MRS ESPOSITO, *the landlady, calls out. The group freezes.*

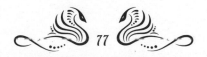

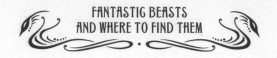

MRS ESPOSITO (*O.S.*)
That you, Tina?

TINA
Yes, Mrs Esposito!

MRS ESPOSITO (*O.S.*)
Are you alone?

TINA
I'm always alone, Mrs Esposito!

A beat.

SCENE 41
INT. GOLDSTEIN RESIDENCE, SITTING ROOM—DUSK

The group enters the Goldstein apartment.

Although impoverished, the apartment is enlivened by workaday magic. An iron is working away on its own in a corner, and a clothes horse revolves clumsily on its wooden legs in front of the fire, drying an assortment of underwear. Magazines are scattered around: The

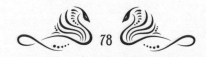

Witch's Friend, Witch Chat *and* Transfiguration Today.

Blonde QUEENIE, *the most beautiful girl ever to don witches' robes, is standing in a silk slip, supervising the mending of a dress on a dressmaker's dummy.* JACOB *is thunderstruck.*

NEWT *barely notices. Impatient to leave as soon as possible, he starts peeking out of the windows.*

QUEENIE
Teenie – you brought men home?

TINA
Gentlemen, this is my sister. You want to put something on, Queenie?

QUEENIE
(unconcerned)
Oh, sure—

She runs her wand up the dummy and the dress runs magically up her body. JACOB *watches the display, dumbfounded.*

TINA, *frustrated, starts tidying the apartment.*

QUEENIE
So, who are they?

TINA
That's Mr Scamander. He's committed a serious infraction of the National Statute of Secrecy—

QUEENIE
(impressed)
He's a *criminal?*

TINA
—uh huh, and this is Mr Kowalski, he's a No-Maj—

QUEENIE
(suddenly worried)
A No-Maj? Teen – what are you up to?

TINA
He's sick – it's a long story – Mr Scamander has lost something, I'm going to help him find it.

JACOB *suddenly staggers, very sweaty and unwell.* QUEENIE *runs to him as* TINA *hovers, also worried.*

QUEENIE
(as JACOB *falls back onto a sofa)*
You need to sit down, honey.
Hey—
(reading his mind)
—he hasn't eaten all day.
And—
(reading his mind)
—aww, that's rough,
(reading his mind)
—he didn't get the money he wanted for his bakery. You bake, honey? I love to cook.

NEWT *is watching* QUEENIE *from his spot by the window, his scientific attention now aroused.*

NEWT
You're a Legilimens?

QUEENIE
Uh huh, yeah. But I always have trouble with your kind. Brits. It's the accent.

JACOB
(cottoning on, appalled)
You know how to read minds?

QUEENIE
Aww, don't worry, honey.
Most guys think what you was
thinking, first time they see me.

QUEENIE *playfully gestures towards* JACOB *with her wand.*

QUEENIE
Now, you need food.

NEWT *looks out the window and sees a Billywig fly past – he's nervous, impatient to get out and find his creatures.*

TINA *and* QUEENIE *busy themselves in the kitchen. Ingredients come floating out of cupboards as* QUEENIE *enchants them into the components of a meal – carrots and apples chop themselves, pastry rolls itself and pans stir.*

QUEENIE
(to TINA*)*
Hot dog . . . again?

TINA
Don't read my mind!

QUEENIE
Not a very wholesome lunch.

TINA *points her wand at the cupboards. Dishes, assorted cutlery and glasses come flying out, setting themselves on the table with a little prodding from* TINA'S *wand.* JACOB, *half-fascinated, half-terrified, staggers towards the table.*

ANGLE ON NEWT, *his hand on the doorknob.*

QUEENIE
(artless)
Hey, Mr Scamander, you
prefer pie or strudel?

All look at NEWT *who, embarrassed, removes his hand from the doorknob.*

NEWT
I really don't have a
preference.

TINA *stares at* NEWT*: confrontational, but also disappointed and hurt.*

JACOB *is already seated at the table, tucking his napkin into his shirt.*

QUEENIE
(reading JACOB'S *mind)*
You prefer strudel, huh,
honey? Strudel it is.

JACOB *nods with excited enthusiasm.* QUEENIE *grins back, delighted.*

With a flick of her wand, QUEENIE *sends raisins, apples and pastry flying into the air. The concoction neatly wraps itself up into a cylindrical pie, baking on the spot, complete with ornate decoration and a dusting of sugar.* JACOB *takes a deep breath in: heaven.*

TINA *lights candles on the table – the meal is ready.*

FOCUS ON NEWT'S *pocket, a small squeak, and* PICKETT *pokes his head out, curious.*

TINA
Well, sit down, Mr
Scamander, we're not going
to poison you.

NEWT, *still hovering near the door, looks somewhat charmed by the situation.* JACOB *glares at him subtly, willing him to sit down.*

SCENE 42
EXT. BROADWAY—NIGHT

CREDENCE *is walking alone through a worldly crowd of late-night diners and theatre-goers. Traffic roars past. He is trying to give out leaflets but is met with only incredulity and faint derision.*

The Woolworth Building looms ahead. CREDENCE *glances towards it with a hint of longing.* GRAVES *stands outside, watching* CREDENCE *intently.* CREDENCE *spots*

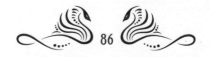

him, hope flickering across his face. Utterly enthralled, CREDENCE *moves across the street towards* GRAVES, *barely looking where he's going – everything else is forgotten.*

SCENE 43
EXT. ALLEYWAY—NIGHT

CREDENCE *stands, head bowed, at the end of a dimly lit alleyway.* GRAVES *joins him, moving in very close to whisper, conspiratorial:*

GRAVES
You're upset. It's your mother again. Somebody's said something – what did they say? Tell me.

CREDENCE
Do you think I'm a freak?

GRAVES
No – I think you're a very special young man or I wouldn't have asked you to help me now, would I?

A pause. GRAVES *rests a hand on* CREDENCE'S *arm. The human contact seems to both startle and captivate* CREDENCE.

GRAVES
Have you any news?

CREDENCE
I'm still looking. Mr Graves,
if I knew whether it was a girl
or boy—

GRAVES
My vision showed only the
child's immense power. He
or she is no older than ten,
and I saw this child in close
proximity to your mother –
she I saw so plainly.

CREDENCE
That could be any one of
hundreds.

GRAVES'S *tone softens – he's beguiling, comforting.*

GRAVES
There is something else.
Something I haven't told you.
I saw you beside me in New

York. You're the one who gains this child's trust. You are the key – I saw this. You want to join the wizarding world. I want those things too, Credence. I want them for you. So find the child. Find the child and we'll all be free.

SCENE 44
INT. GOLDSTEIN RESIDENCE, SITTING ROOM—HALF AN HOUR LATER—NIGHT

The catch on NEWT'S *case pops open.* NEWT *reaches down and pushes it shut.*

JACOB *looks a little better for having eaten. He and* QUEENIE *are getting on famously.*

QUEENIE
The job ain't that glamorous. I mean, I spend most days making coffee, unjinxing the john … Tina's the career girl.

(she reads his mind)
Nah. We're orphans. Ma and Pa died of dragon pox when we were kids. Aww …
(reading his mind)
You're sweet. But we got each other!

JACOB
Could you stop reading my mind for a second? Don't get me wrong – I love it.

QUEENIE *giggles, delighted, captivated by* JACOB.

JACOB
This meal – it's insanely good! This is what I do – I'm a cook and this is, like, the greatest meal I have ever had in my life.

QUEENIE
(laughing)
Oh you slay me! I ain't never really talked to a No-Maj before.

JACOB
Really?

QUEENIE *and* JACOB *gaze into each other's eyes.* NEWT *and* TINA *sit opposite each other, uncomfortably silent in the presence of such affectionate behaviour.*

QUEENIE
(to TINA*)*
I am not flirting!

TINA
(embarrassed)
I'm just saying – don't go getting attached, he's going to have to be Obliviated!
(to JACOB*)*
It's nothing personal.

JACOB *is suddenly very pale and sweaty again, although still trying to look good for* QUEENIE.

QUEENIE
(to JACOB*)*
Oh, hey, you okay, honey?

NEWT *briskly gets up from the table and awkwardly stands behind his chair.*

NEWT
Miss Goldstein, I think Mr Kowalski could do with an early night. And besides, you

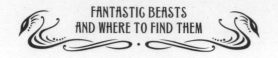

and I will need to be up early
tomorrow morning to find
my Niffler, so—

QUEENIE
(to TINA*)*
What's a Niffler?

TINA *looks put out.*

TINA
Don't ask.
(moving towards a back room)
Okay, you guys can bunk in
here.

<u>SCENE 45</u>
INT. GOLDSTEIN RESIDENCE, BEDROOM—NIGHT

The boys are tucked up in neatly made twin beds. NEWT *is resolutely turned away on his side, while* JACOB *is sitting up in bed, trying to make sense of a wizarding book.*

TINA, *wearing patterned blue pyjamas, tentatively knocks*

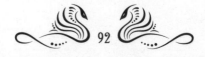

on the door, and enters carrying a tray of cocoa. The mugs are stirring themselves – JACOB *is captivated again.*

TINA

I thought you might like a hot drink?

TINA *carefully hands* JACOB *his mug.* NEWT *remains turned away, feigning sleep, so* TINA, *with some frustration, pointedly places his cup on the bedside table.*

JACOB

Hey, Mr Scamander—

(to NEWT, *trying to make him friendlier)*

Look, cocoa!

NEWT *does not move.*

TINA

(irritated)

The toilet's down the hall to the right.

JACOB

Thanks …

As TINA *shuts the door,* JACOB *gets a quick glimpse of* QUEENIE *in the other room, wearing a much less demure dressing gown.*

JACOB

Very much . . .

The moment the door closes NEWT *jumps up, still wearing his overcoat, and places his case on the floor. To* JACOB'S *utter astonishment,* NEWT *opens the case and walks down inside it, now completely out of sight.*

JACOB *lets out a small scream of alarm.*

NEWT'S *hand appears from the case, beckoning him imperiously.* JACOB *stares, breathing heavily, trying to process the situation.*

NEWT'S *hand, impatient, appears again.*

NEWT (*O.S.*)

Come on.

JACOB *rallies himself, gets out of bed and steps down into* NEWT'S *case. However, he gets stuck at his waistline and tries hard to squeeze himself through, the case bouncing up and down with his efforts.*

JACOB

For the love of . . .

With a final frustrated jump, JACOB *suddenly disappears through the case, which snaps shut after him.*

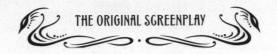

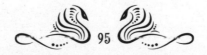

SCENE 46
INT. NEWT'S CASE—A MOMENT LATER—NIGHT

JACOB *crashes down the steps of the case, colliding with various objects, instruments and bottles as he goes.*

He finds himself inside a small wooden shed containing a camp bed, tropical gear and various tools hung up on the walls. Wooden cupboards contain rope, nets and collecting jars. A very old typewriter, a pile of manuscripts and a medieval bestiary sit on a desk. Potted plants line a shelf. Rows of pills and tablets, syringes and vials form a medicine chest, and tacked up on the walls are notes, maps,

drawings and a few moving photographs of extraordinary creatures. A dried carcass hangs from a hook. Several sacks of feed are resting against the wall.

NEWT
(*glances at* JACOB)
Will you sit down.

JACOB *drops onto a crate hand-labelled MOONCALF PELLETS.*

JACOB
That's good.

NEWT *moves forward to examine the bite on* JACOB'S *neck – one quick glance.*

NEWT
Ah, that's definitely the Murtlap. You must be particularly susceptible. See, you're a Muggle. So our physiologies are subtly different.

NEWT *busies himself at his work station, using plants and the contents of various bottles to create a poultice, which he rapidly applies to* JACOB'S *neck.*

JACOB
Eww . . .

NEWT

Now stay still. Now that should stop the sweating.

(handing him some pills)

And one of those should sort the twitch.

JACOB *looks suspiciously at the pills in his hand. Finally, deciding he has nothing to lose, he swallows them.*

ANGLE ON NEWT, *who has now removed his waistcoat, undone his bow tie and lowered his braces. He picks up a meat cleaver and hacks chunks of meat off a large carcass, before tossing them into a bucket.*

NEWT

(handing him the bucket)

Take that.

JACOB *looks disgusted.* NEWT *doesn't notice, his attention now focused on a spiny cocoon, which he slowly begins to squeeze. As he does so, the cocoon emits a luminous venom, which* NEWT *collects into a glass vial.*

NEWT

(to the cocoon)

Come on . . .

JACOB

What you got there?

NEWT
Well this – the locals call 'Swooping Evil' – not the friendliest of names. It's quite an agile fellow.

As if to demonstrate, NEWT *flicks the cocoon, which unravels, dangling elegantly from his finger.*

NEWT
I've been studying him. And I am pretty sure his venom could be quite useful if properly diluted. Just to remove bad memories, you know.

Quite suddenly NEWT *throws the Swooping Evil towards* JACOB. *The creature bursts out from its cocoon – a bat-like, spikey and colourful creature – which howls in* JACOB'S *face before* NEWT *recalls it.* JACOB *recoils dramatically, but this was evidently* NEWT'S *idea of a little joke …*

NEWT
(smiling to himself)
Probably shouldn't let him loose in here, though.

NEWT *opens the door of his shed and walks through.*

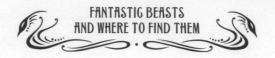

NEWT

Come on.

JACOB*, now thoroughly startled, follows him out.*

SCENE 47

INT. NEWT'S CASE, ANIMAL AREA—DAY

The perimeter of the leather case is dimly visible, but the place has swollen to the size of a small aircraft hangar. It contains what appears to be a safari park in miniature. Each of NEWT'S *creatures has its own perfect, magically realised, habitat.*

JACOB *steps into this world, totally amazed.*

NEWT *is standing in the nearest habitat – a slice of Arizona desert. This area contains* FRANK*, a magnificent Thunderbird – a creature like a large albatross, his glorious wings shimmering with cloud- and sun-like patterns. One of his legs is rubbed raw and bloody – he has obviously previously been chained. As* FRANK *flaps his wings, his habitat fills with a torrential downpour, thunder and lightning.* NEWT *uses his wand to create a magical umbrella, shielding him from the rain.*

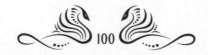

NEWT
(eyes on FRANK *up high)*
Come on ... come on ...
down you come ... come on.

Slowly FRANK *calms himself, lowering down to stand on a large rock in front of* NEWT. *As he does, the rain dies down and is replaced by a brilliant, hot sunshine.*

NEWT *puts his wand away and produces a handful of grubs from his pocket.* FRANK *watches intently.*

NEWT *strokes* FRANK *with his free hand, calming him, affectionate.*

NEWT
Oh, thank Paracelsus. If you'd
have got out that could have
been quite catastrophic.
(to JACOB*)*
You see, he's the real reason
I came to America. To bring
Frank home.

JACOB, *still staring, steps slowly forwards. In reaction,* FRANK *starts to flap his wings, agitated.*

NEWT
(to JACOB*)*
No sorry – stay there – he's a

wee bit sensitive to strangers.
(*to* FRANK, *calming)*
Here you are – here you are.
(*to* JACOB)
He was trafficked, you see. I found him in Egypt, he was all chained up. Couldn't leave him there, had to bring him back. I'm going to put you back where you belong, aren't I, Frank. To the wilds of Arizona.

NEWT, *his face full of hope and expectation, hugs* FRANK'S *head. Then, grinning, he casts the handful of grubs high into the air.* FRANK *soars majestically upwards after them, sunlight bursting from his wings.*

NEWT *watches him fly with love and pride. Then he turns, puts his hands to his mouth, and roars beast-like towards another area of the case.*

NEWT *moves past* JACOB, *grabbing the bucket of meat.* JACOB *stumbles after him as several Doxys buzz around his head.* JACOB, *dazed, swats them out of the way. Behind him a large dung beetle rolls a giant ball of dung.*

We hear NEWT *roar loudly again.* JACOB *hurries towards the sound, finding* NEWT *in a sandy, moonlit territory.*

NEWT
(under his breath)
Ah – here they come.

JACOB
Here who comes?

NEWT
The Graphorns.

A large creature comes charging into sight: a Graphorn – built like a sabre-toothed tiger but with slimy tentacles at its mouth. JACOB *screams and tries to back off, but* NEWT *grabs hold of his arm, stopping him.*

NEWT
You're all right. You're all right.

The Graphorn moves closer to NEWT.

NEWT
(stroking the Graphorn)
Hello, hello!

The Graphorn's strange slimy tentacles rest on NEWT'S *shoulder, seeming to embrace him.*

NEWT
So they're the last breeding

pair in existence. If I hadn't managed to rescue them, that could have been the end of Graphorns – for ever.

A younger Graphorn trots straight up to JACOB *and begins licking his hand, circling him curiously. He stares down at it, then gently reaches out and strokes its head.* NEWT *watches* JACOB, *pleased.*

NEWT

All right.

NEWT *throws a piece of meat into the enclosure, which is hastily chased and consumed by the young Graphorn.*

JACOB

So what – you, you rescue these creatures?

NEWT

Yes, that's right. Rescue, nurture and protect them, and I'm gently trying to educate my fellow wizards about them.

A tiny bright pink bird, the Fwooper, flies past and comes to rest on a little perch, suspended from mid-air.

NEWT *heads up a small ramp of stairs.*

NEWT
(*to* JACOB)
Come on.

They enter a bamboo wood, ducking and diving through the trees. NEWT *calls out.*

JACOB
Wow!

NEWT
Titus? Finn? Poppy, Marlow, Tom?

They emerge into a sunlit glade, NEWT *producing* PICKETT *from his pocket and holding him perched on his hand.*

NEWT
(*to* JACOB)
He had a cold. He needed some body warmth.

JACOB
Aww.

They move towards a small tree bathed in sunlight. At their approach, a clan of Bowtruckles chatters and rushes out of the leaves.

NEWT *extends his arm towards the tree, trying to persuade* PICKETT *to rejoin the others. The Bowtruckles clack noisily when they see* PICKETT.

NEWT
Right, on you hop.

PICKETT *steadfastly refuses to leave* NEWT'S *arm.*

NEWT
(*to* JACOB)
See, he has some attachment issues.
(*to* PICKETT)
Now come on, Pickett. Pickett. No, they're not going to bully you ... now, come on. Pickett!

PICKETT *clings by his spindly hands to one of* NEWT'S *fingers, desperate not to return to the tree.* NEWT *finally resigns himself.*

NEWT
All right. But that is exactly why they accuse me of favouritism ...

NEWT *puts* PICKETT *onto his shoulder and turns. On seeing a large, round, empty nest, he looks concerned.*

NEWT
I wonder where Dougal's gone.

From within a nearby nest, we hear chirping sounds.

NEWT
All right I'm coming … I'm coming, Mum's here – Mum's here.

NEWT *reaches into the nest and scoops up a baby Occamy.*

NEWT
Ah – hello you – let me take a look at you.

JACOB
I know these guys.

NEWT
New Occamy.
(*to* JACOB)
Your Occamy.

JACOB
What do you mean? My Occamy?

NEWT
Yes – do you want to …

NEWT *proffers the Occamy to* JACOB.

JACOB
Oh wow . . . yeah, sure.
Okay . . . ah ha.

JACOB *holds the newborn creature gently in his hands and stares. As he moves to stroke its head, the Occamy moves to nip him.* JACOB *starts backwards.*

NEWT
Ah, no, sorry – don't pet
them. They learn to defend
themselves early. See, their
shells are made of silver so
they're incredibly valuable.

NEWT *feeds the other babies in the nest.*

JACOB
Okay . . .

NEWT
Their nests tend to get
ransacked by hunters.

NEWT, *delighted by* JACOB'S *interest in his creatures, takes back the baby Occamy, placing it in the nest.*

JACOB
Thank you.
(croaky)
Mr Scamander?

NEWT
Call me Newt.

JACOB
Newt . . . I don't think I'm dreaming.

NEWT
(vaguely amused)
What gave it away?

JACOB
I ain't got the brains to make this up.

NEWT *looks at* JACOB, *both intrigued and flattered.*

NEWT
Actually, would you mind throwing some of those pellets in with the Mooncalves over there?

JACOB
Yeah, sure.

JACOB *bends down and picks up the bucket of pellets.*

NEWT
Just over there . . .

NEWT *grabs a nearby wheelbarrow and sets off further into the case.*

NEWT
(annoyed)
Bugger – Niffler's gone. Of course he has, little bugger. Any chance to get his hands on something shiny.

As JACOB *walks through the case, we see what appear to be golden 'leaves' falling from a tiny tree, which move together en masse towards the camera. They swarm upwards, mingling with Doxys, Glow Bugs and Grindylows which float through the air.*

THE CAMERA PANS UP to reveal another magnificent creature, the Nundu – looking almost exactly like a lion, it has a large mane which bursts forth when it roars. It stands proudly on a large rock, roaring at the moon. NEWT *scatters food at its feet and purposefully moves on.*

A Diricawl – a small, plump bird – waddles in the foreground followed by its constantly Apparating chicks, as JACOB *climbs up a steep grassy bank.*

JACOB
(to himself)
What did you do today, Jacob? I was inside a suitcase.

At the top, JACOB *finds a large moonlit rock face populated by little Mooncalves – shy, with huge eyes filling their whole faces.*

JACOB
Hey! Oh, hello fellas – all right – all right.

The Mooncalves jump and hop down the rocks towards JACOB, *who finds himself suddenly surrounded by their friendly, hopeful faces.*

JACOB
Take it easy – take it easy.

As he throws pellets, the Mooncalves bob eagerly up and down. JACOB *visibly seems to be feeling better – he really likes this …*

ANGLE ON NEWT, *now cradling a luminescent creature with sprouting alien-like tendrils. He feeds the creature with a bottle, while carefully watching how* JACOB *handles the Mooncalves – he recognises a kindred spirit.*

JACOB
(still feeding the Mooncalves)
There you go, cutie. Ah, there it is.

A kind of icy cry echoes from nearby.

JACOB
(*towards* NEWT)
Did you hear that?

But NEWT *is gone.* JACOB *turns to see a curtain billowing open, behind which is revealed a snowscape.*

We push inwards, towards a small oleaginous black mass suspended in mid-air – an Obscurus. JACOB, *intrigued, moves into the snowscape to get a closer look. The mass continues to swirl, emitting a disturbed, restless energy.* JACOB *reaches out to touch it.*

NEWT (*O.S.*)
(*sharp*)
Step back.

JACOB *jumps.*

JACOB
Jeez . . .

NEWT
Step back . . .

JACOB
What's the matter with this?

NEWT
I said step away.

JACOB
What the hell is this thing?

NEWT
It's an Obscurus.

JACOB *looks at* NEWT, *who is momentarily lost in a bad reverie.* NEWT *turns abruptly away and heads back towards the hut, his tone colder, more efficient, no longer happy to play about in the case.*

NEWT
I need to get going, find everyone who's escaped before they get hurt.

The pair enters another forest, NEWT *ploughing ahead, on a mission.*

JACOB
Before *they* could get hurt?

NEWT
Yes, Mr Kowalski. See, they're currently in alien terrain, surrounded by millions of the most vicious creatures on the planet.

(*a beat*)
Humans.

NEWT *stops once more, staring into a large savannah enclosure, which is empty of any beasts.*

NEWT
So where would you say that a medium-sized creature that likes broad, open plains – trees – water holes – that kind of thing – where might she go?

JACOB
In New York City?

NEWT
Yes.

JACOB
Plains?

JACOB *shrugs as he tries to think of somewhere.*

JACOB
Ah – Central Park?

NEWT
And where is that exactly?

JACOB
Where is Central Park?

A beat.

JACOB
Well look, I would come and show you, but, don't you think it's kind of a double cross? The girls take us in – they make us hot cocoa …

NEWT
You do realise that when they see you've stopped sweating, they'll Obliviate you in a heartbeat.

JACOB
What does 'Bliviate' mean?

NEWT
It'll be like you wake up and all memory of magic is gone.

JACOB
I won't remember any of this?

He looks around. This world is extraordinary.

NEWT

No.

JACOB

All right, yeah – okay – I'll help you.

NEWT

(picking up a bucket)

Come on, then.

SCENE 48
EXT./INT. STREET OUTSIDE SECOND SALEM CHURCH—NIGHT

CREDENCE *walks home towards the church. He looks happier than before: his meeting with* GRAVES *has comforted him.*

CREDENCE *slowly enters the church, shutting the double doors quietly.*

CHASTITY *is in the kitchen area, drying crockery.*

MARY LOU *sits in semi-darkness on the stairs.* CREDENCE *senses her and pauses, his face one of trepidation.*

MARY LOU
Credence – where have you been?

CREDENCE
I was ... looking for a place for tomorrow's meeting. There's a corner on Thirty-second that could—

CREDENCE *moves round to the bottom of the stairs, falling silent at the severe expression on* MARY LOU'S *face.*

CREDENCE
I'm sorry, Ma. I didn't realise it was so late.

As if on autopilot, CREDENCE *removes his belt.* MARY LOU *stands and extends her hand, taking the belt. In silence, she turns and walks up the stairs,* CREDENCE *obediently following.*

MODESTY *moves to the bottom of the stairs, watching them go, a look of fear and upset on her face.*

SCENE 49
EXT. CENTRAL PARK—NIGHT

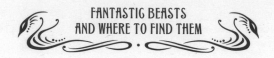

A large frozen pond in the middle of Central Park. Children ice-skate. A boy takes a tumble. A girl comes to help him up, they link hands.

As they are about to stand, a light becomes visible underneath the ice. A deep rumbling sound echoes. The children stare as a glowing beast glides under the ice beneath them, and off into the distance.

SCENE 50
EXT. DIAMOND DISTRICT—NIGHT

NEWT *and* JACOB *walk along another deserted street on the way to Central Park. The shops around them are full of expensive jewellery, diamonds, precious stones.* NEWT, *carrying his case, scans the shadows for small movements.*

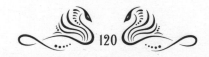

NEWT
I was watching you at dinner.

JACOB
Yeah.

NEWT
People like you, don't they, Mr Kowalski.

JACOB
(startled)
Oh – well, I'm – I'm sure people like you, too – huh?

NEWT
(not very concerned)
No, not really. I annoy people.

JACOB
(not sure how to answer)
Ah.

NEWT *seems thoroughly intrigued by* JACOB.

NEWT
Why did you decide to be a baker?

JACOB
Ah, well, um – because I'm dying – in that canning factory.
(off NEWT'S *look)*
Everyone there's dying. It just crushes the life outta you. You like canned food?

NEWT
No.

JACOB
Me neither. That's why I want to make pastries, you know. It makes people happy. We're going this way.

JACOB *heads off to his right.* NEWT *follows.*

NEWT
So did you get your loan?

JACOB
Er, no – I ain't got no collateral. Stayed in the army too long, apparently – I don't know.

NEWT
What, you fought in the war?

JACOB
Of course I fought in the war, everyone fought in the war – you didn't fight in the war?

NEWT
I worked mostly with dragons, Ukrainian Ironbellies – Eastern Front.

NEWT *suddenly stops. He has noticed a small shiny earring lying on top of a car bonnet. His eyes move downwards: diamonds are scattered across the pavement, leading towards the window of one particular diamond shop.*

NEWT *stealthily follows the trail, creeping past shop windows. Something catches his eye and suddenly he pauses. Very slowly, he tiptoes backwards.*

The Niffler is standing in a shop window. In order to hide, it is emulating a jewellery stand, little arms outstretched, covered in diamonds.

NEWT *stares at the Niffler in disbelief. Sensing* NEWT'S *stare, the Niffler slowly turns. The two of them make eye contact.*

A beat.

Suddenly the Niffler is off: scurrying further into the shop and away from NEWT. NEWT *whips out his wand.*

NEWT

Finestra.

The window glass shatters and NEWT *leaps inside, seizing at drawers and cupboards, desperate to find the creature.* JACOB *stares down the street, incredulous as he watches* NEWT *who, from an outsider's perspective, appears to be looting the diamond shop.*

The Niffler appears, scurrying over NEWT'S *shoulders in an attempt to get higher and away from his clutches.* NEWT *jumps onto a desk after him, but the Niffler is now balancing on a crystal chandelier.*

NEWT *reaches out and trips, both he and the Niffler now hanging from the chandelier as it swings wildly round and round.*

JACOB *looks around the street nervously, checking if anyone else can hear the chaos coming from within the shop.*

Finally the chandelier crashes to the floor, smashing. Straight away the Niffler is back up, clambering across cases full of jewellery, NEWT *in hot pursuit.*

A catch opens on NEWT'S *case and a roar comes from within.* JACOB *fearfully looks towards the case.*

The Niffler and NEWT *continue their chase, finally climbing onto a jewellery case that can't take their weight. The case, with them both on top, falls to rest against one of the shop windows. Both* NEWT *and the Niffler become very still . . .*

JACOB *breathes deeply and slowly moves forward to close the latch on the case.*

Suddenly a crack appears on the window. NEWT *watches as the crack spreads across the pane of glass and the window bursts open, shattering across the pavement –* NEWT *and the Niffler crashing to the ground.*

The Niffler is still only for a moment before running off down the street. NEWT *quickly gathers himself, drawing his wand.*

NEWT

ACCIO!

IN SLOW MOTION the Niffler sails backwards through the air towards NEWT. *As he flies, he looks sideways at the most glorious window display yet. His eyes widen. Jewellery falls from his pouch as he flies towards* NEWT *and* JACOB, *who duck and dive as they run forwards towards the creature.*

Passing a lamp-post, the Niffler stretches out an arm, spinning around the pole and flying onwards, out of the trajectory

NEWT *had him on, and towards the glorious window.* NEWT *casts a spell towards the window, turning it into a sticky jelly, which finally traps the Niffler.*

NEWT
(to the Niffler)
All right? Happy?

NEWT, *now covered in jewellery, pulls the Niffler from the window.*

We hear police sirens in the background.

NEWT
One down, two to go.

Police cars come racing through the streets.

NEWT *once again sets about shaking all the diamonds from the Niffler's pocket.*

The police cars pull up, and POLICEMEN *run out, guns aimed at* NEWT *and* JACOB. JACOB, *also covered in jewels, holds up his hands in surrender.*

JACOB
They went that way, officer …

POLICE OFFICER 1
Hands up!

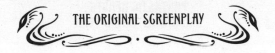

The Niffler, stuffed into NEWT'S *overcoat, pokes out its little nose and squeaks.*

POLICE OFFICER 2
What the hell is THAT?

JACOB *suddenly looks to the left, his face one of terror.*

JACOB
(barely able to speak)
Lion . . .

A beat and then, in unison, the police turn both their eyes and their guns towards the other end of the street.

Perplexed, NEWT *looks too . . . a lion is stalking towards them.*

NEWT
(calm)
You know, New York is considerably more interesting than I'd expected.

Before the police can look back, NEWT *grabs* JACOB *and they Disapparate.*

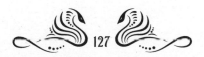

SCENE 51
EXT. CENTRAL PARK—NIGHT

NEWT *and* JACOB *hurry through the frost-covered park.*

As they cross a bridge, they are almost bowled over by an ostrich, which tears past them, running for its life.

A loud rumble can be heard in the distance.

NEWT *tugs protective headgear out of his pocket, and hands it to* JACOB.

NEWT
Put this on.

JACOB
Why – why would I have to wear something like this?

NEWT
Because your skull is susceptible to breakage under immense force.

NEWT *runs on. Utterly terrified,* JACOB *puts on the hat and chases after* NEWT.

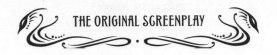

SCENE 52
EXT. GOLDSTEIN RESIDENCE—NIGHT

TINA *and* QUEENIE *lean out of their bedroom window, craning into the dark. Another bellowing roar reverberates through the winter night. Other windows open, neighbours stare sleepily over the city.*

SCENE 53
INT. GOLDSTEIN RESIDENCE—NIGHT

TINA *and* QUEENIE *burst into the bedroom where* JACOB *and* NEWT *are meant to be asleep. Every trace of the two men has gone. Furious,* TINA *storms off to dress.* QUEENIE *looks upset.*

QUEENIE
But we made 'em cocoa . . .

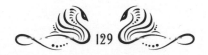

SCENE 54
EXT. CENTRAL PARK ZOO—NIGHT

NEWT *and* JACOB *run up to the now half-empty zoo, the outer walls of which have been demolished in places. A large pile of rubble lies at the entrance.*

Another bellowing roar echoes around the brick building. NEWT *produces a body protector.*

NEWT
Okay, if you just, uh, pop this on.

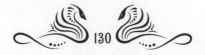

NEWT *stands behind* JACOB, *fastening the breastplate over him.*

JACOB
Okay.

NEWT
Now there's absolutely nothing for you to worry about.

JACOB
Tell me – has anyone ever believed you when you told them not to worry?

NEWT
My philosophy is that worrying means you suffer twice.

JACOB *digests* NEWT'S *'wisdom'.*

NEWT *picks up his case and* JACOB *follows him, stumbling over rubble and debris.*

They stand at the entrance to the zoo. A loud snort comes from within.

NEWT
She's in season. She needs to mate.

ANGLE ON the Erumpent – a large, rotund, rhino-like creature with a massive horn protruding from her forehead. Five times his size, she is nuzzling up against the enclosure of a terrified hippo.

NEWT *takes out a tiny vial of liquid – he pulls the stopper out with his teeth and spits it to the side before dabbing a spot of the liquid onto each wrist.* JACOB *looks at him – the smell is pungent.*

NEWT
Erumpent musk – she is mad for it.

NEWT *passes* JACOB *the open bottle and heads into the zoo.*

TIME CUT:

NEWT *places his case down on the ground near the Erumpent and slowly, seductively, opens it.*

He begins to perform a 'mating ritual' – a series of grunts, wiggles, rolls and groans – to gain the Erumpent's attention.

Finally the Erumpent turns away from the hippo – she is interested in NEWT. *They face each other, circle round, undulating weirdly. The Erumpent's demeanour is puppy-like, her horn glowing orange.*

NEWT *rolls along the floor – the Erumpent copies, moving nearer and nearer to the open case.*

NEWT
Good girl – come on – into
the case . . .

JACOB *takes a sniff of the Erumpent musk. As he does so, a fish flies through the air and jolts him, spilling the musk.*

The wind changes. Trees rustle. The Erumpent takes a deep breath in – she can smell the new, more powerful aroma coming from JACOB.

JACOB *looks around. A seal sits behind him looking guilty, before cheekily running away.*

When JACOB *turns back, he sees the Erumpent is now on her feet, staring at him.*

ANGLE ON NEWT *and* JACOB, *realising what is about to happen.*

BACK TO SCENE:

The Erumpent charges towards the source of the smell, bellowing madly. JACOB *wails, running as fast as he can in the opposite direction. The Erumpent gives chase – they crash through rubble and ice-ponds, before charging across the snow-covered park.*

NEWT *draws his wand—*

NEWT
Repar—

Before he can finish, his wand is whipped out of his hand by a baboon, which runs off, clutching its prize.

NEWT
Merlin's beard!

ANGLE ON JACOB*, tanking along, the Erumpent close behind him.*

ANGLE ON NEWT*, face to face with the curious baboon, which examines his wand.*

NEWT *breaks a bit of twig from a branch and holds it out, trying to persuade the baboon to trade with him.*

NEWT
They're exactly the same . . .
same thing.

BACK TO JACOB:

In trying to climb a tree, JACOB *has ended up hanging precariously upside down from a branch.*

JACOB
(bellowing, terrified)
Newt!

We see the Erumpent below him. She lies on her back, wiggling her legs in the air invitingly.

ANGLE BACK ON NEWT *– the baboon shakes* NEWT'S *wand.*

NEWT
No, no, no, don't!

NEWT *looks worried – BANG – the wand 'goes off', the spell knocking the baboon backwards. The wand flies back to* NEWT.

NEWT
I'm so sorry—

ANGLE ON JACOB *– the Erumpent is now on her feet. She charges towards the tree, digging her horn deep into the trunk. The tree bubbles with glowing liquid before exploding and crashing to the ground.*

JACOB *is thrown off, rolling down a steep, snowy hill and onto the frozen lake below.*

The Erumpent charges after him, hits the ice and skids. NEWT *comes careering down the hill, also hitting the ice. He performs an athletic slide, his case open – the Erumpent is mere feet from* JACOB *when the case swallows her.*

NEWT
Good show, Mr Kowalski!

JACOB *holds out his hand to shake.*

JACOB
Call me Jacob.

They shake hands.

THIRD PERSON POV: Someone watches as NEWT *hauls* JACOB *up and they slip and slide across the frozen lake as fast as they can.*

NEWT
Well, two down, one to go.

HOLD ON TINA *as she hides on the bridge above them, peeking down.*

NEWT (*O.S.*)
(*to* JACOB)
In you hop.

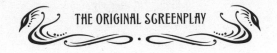

We see the case sitting alone below the bridge.

TINA *quickly appears around the corner and hurriedly sits on the case. She closes the catches, looking shocked but determined.*

ANNOUNCER (*V.O.*)
Ladies and gentlemen . . .

SCENE 55
INT. CITY HALL—NIGHT

A large ornately decorated hall, covered in patriotic emblems. Hundreds of glamorously dressed people sit at round tables, looking towards a stage at the far end. Over this stage hangs a large poster of SENATOR SHAW *with a slogan reading 'America's Future'.*

An ANNOUNCER *stands behind the microphone.*

ANNOUNCER
. . . now tonight's keynote speaker needs no introduction from me. He's been mentioned as a future

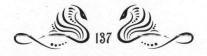

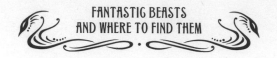

President – and if you don't believe me, just read his daddy's newspapers—

Indulgent laughter from the crowd. We see SHAW SR *and* LANGDON *seated at a table, surrounded by the crème de la crème of New York society.*

ANNOUNCER
—ladies and gentlemen, I give you the Senator for New York, Henry Shaw!

Tumultuous applause. SENATOR SHAW *bounds forwards, acknowledging the cheers, pointing and winking at intimates in the crowd, and mounts the steps.*

<u>SCENE 56</u>
EXT. DARK STREET—NIGHT

Something is streaking through the streets, too large and fast for a human. Strange, laboured breathing and snarling – it is inhuman, beast-like.

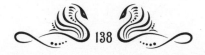

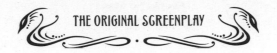

SCENE 57
EXT. STREET NEAR CITY HALL—NIGHT

TINA *is hurrying along, clutching the case. Street lights start going out around her. She stops, feels something pass in the darkness – turns, staring, scared.*

SCENE 58
INT. CITY HALL—NIGHT

SENATOR SHAW
. . . and it's true we have made some progress, but there is no reward for idleness. So just as the odious saloons have been banished . . .

A strange, haunting noise comes from the organ pipes at the back of the room. Everyone turns to look, the SENATOR *pauses.*

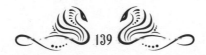

SENATOR SHAW
... so now the pool halls, and
these private parlours ...

The strange noise gets louder.

Guests turn to look again. The SENATOR *seems anxious. People mutter.*

Suddenly something explodes forth from underneath the organ. Something huge and bestial, although invisible, is soaring down the hall – tables fly, people are thrown, lights smash and people scream as it carves a line towards the stage.

SENATOR SHAW *is thrown backwards against his own poster, raised up high and suspended for a moment in mid-air before being brought down with a violent crash – dead.*

The 'beast' rips at his poster – a frenzied slashing with harsh, noisy breathing – before swarming back out from where it came.

Sounds of anguish and panic from the crowd as SHAW SR *fights through the debris towards his son's torn and bleeding body.*

ANGLE ON SENATOR SHAW'S *body, his face brutally scarred.* SHAW SR *looks devastated as he crouches beside his son.*

ANGLE ON LANGDON, *now on his feet, slightly drunk. Determined, perhaps triumphant.*

LANGDON

Witches!

SCENE 59

INT. MACUSA LOBBY—NIGHT

Focus on the gigantic dial showing the MAGICAL EXPOSURE THREAT LEVEL. The hand moves from SEVERE to EMERGENCY.

TINA, *case in hand, runs up the lobby steps, past witches and wizards huddled in groups, whispering nervously.*

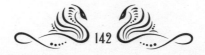

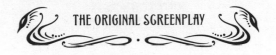

HEINRICH EBERSTADT (*V.O.*)
Our American friends have permitted a breach of the Statute of Secrecy . . .

SCENE 60
INT. PENTAGRAM OFFICE—NIGHT

An impressive hall arranged like an old parliament debating chamber. Every seat is occupied by wizards from all parts of the world. MADAM PICQUERY *is presiding,* GRAVES *at her side.*

The Swiss delegate is speaking.

HEINRICH EBERSTADT
. . . that threatens to expose us all.

MADAM PICQUERY
I will not be lectured by the man who let Gellert Grindelwald slip through his fingers—

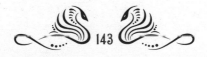

A hologram image of SENATOR SHAW'S *dead and twisted body floats high above the room, emitting a glowing light.*

All heads turn as TINA *hurries into the chamber.*

TINA
Madam President, I'm so sorry to interrupt, but this is critical—

Echoing silence. TINA *slides to a halt in the middle of the marble floor before realising exactly what she's walked into. The delegates stare at her.*

MADAM PICQUERY
You'd better have an excellent excuse for this intrusion, Miss Goldstein.

TINA
Yes – I do.
(stepping forwards to address her)
Ma'am. Yesterday a wizard entered New York with a case. *This* case full of magical creatures, and – unfortunately – some have escaped.

MADAM PICQUERY

He arrived yesterday? You have known for twenty-four hours that an unregistered wizard set magical beasts loose in New York and you see fit to tell us only when a man has been killed?

TINA

Who has been killed?

MADAM PICQUERY

Where is this man?

TINA *sets the case flat on the floor and thumps the lid. After a second or two, it creaks open. First* NEWT, *then* JACOB *emerge, looking sheepish and nervous.*

BRITISH ENVOY

Scamander?

NEWT

(closing the case)

Oh – er – hello, Minister.

MOMOLU WOTORSON

Theseus Scamander? The war hero?

BRITISH ENVOY
No, this is his little brother. And what are you doing in New York?

NEWT
I came to buy an Appaloosa Puffskein, sir.

BRITISH ENVOY
(suspicious)
Right. What are you really doing here?

MADAM PICQUERY
(to TINA, *about* JACOB*)*
Goldstein – and who is this?

TINA
This is Jacob Kowalski, Madam President, he's a No-Maj who got bitten by one of Mr Scamander's creatures.

Furious reaction from the MACUSA employees and dignitaries all around.

MINISTERS
(*whispers*)
No-Maj? Obliviated?

NEWT *is absorbed in the image of* SENATOR SHAW'S *body floating around the room.*

NEWT
Merlin's beard!

MADAM YA ZHOU
You know which of your creatures was responsible, Mr Scamander?

NEWT
No creature did this . . . don't pretend! You must know what that was, look at the marks . . .

ANGLE ON SENATOR SHAW'S *face.*

ANGLE ON NEWT.

NEWT
That was an Obscurus.

Mass consternation, muttering, exclamations. GRAVES *looks alert.*

MADAM PICQUERY
You go too far, Mr Scamander. There is no Obscurial in America. Impound that case, Graves!

GRAVES *summons the case; it lands next to him.* NEWT *draws his wand.*

NEWT
(*to* GRAVES)
No . . . give that b—!

MADAM PICQUERY
Arrest them!

A dazzling eruption of spells hit NEWT, TINA *and* JACOB, *all of whom are slammed to their knees.* NEWT'S *wand flies out of his hand, caught by* GRAVES.

GRAVES *stands and picks up the case.*

NEWT
(*magically restrained*)
No – no – don't hurt those creatures – please, you don't understand – nothing in there is dangerous, nothing!

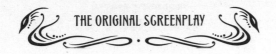

MADAM PICQUERY
We'll be the judges of that!
(to the Aurors now standing behind them)
Take them to the cells!

ANGLE ON GRAVES *watching* TINA *as she,* NEWT *and* JACOB *are dragged away.*

NEWT
(screaming, desperate)
Don't hurt those creatures – there is nothing in there that is dangerous. Please don't hurt my creatures – they are not dangerous ... please, they are not dangerous!

SCENE 61
INT. MACUSA CELL—DAY

NEWT, TINA *and* JACOB *sitting,* NEWT *with his head in his hands, still in utter despair about his creatures. Finally* TINA, *on the verge of tears, breaks the silence.*

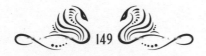

TINA
I am so sorry about your creatures, Mr Scamander. I truly am.

NEWT *remains silent.*

JACOB
(sotto voce, to TINA*)*
Can someone please tell me what this Obscurial Obscurius thing is? Please?

TINA
(also sotto voce)
There hasn't been one for centuries—

NEWT
I met one in Sudan three months ago. There used to be more of them but they still exist. Before wizards went underground, when we were still being hunted by Muggles, young wizards and witches sometimes tried to suppress their magic to avoid persecution. Instead of learning to

harness or to control their powers, they developed what was called an Obscurus.

TINA
(*off* JACOB'S *confusion*)
It's an unstable, uncontrollable dark force that busts out and – and attacks … and then vanishes …

As she talks, we see the penny dropping. An Obscurus fits everything she knows about the perpetrator of the New York attacks.

TINA
(*to* NEWT)
Obscurials can't survive long, can they?

NEWT
There's no documented case of any Obscurial surviving past the age of ten. The one I met in Africa was eight when she – she was eight when she died.

JACOB
What are you telling me here – that Senator Shaw was killed by a – by a *kid*?

NEWT'S *look says 'yes'.*

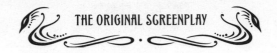

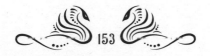

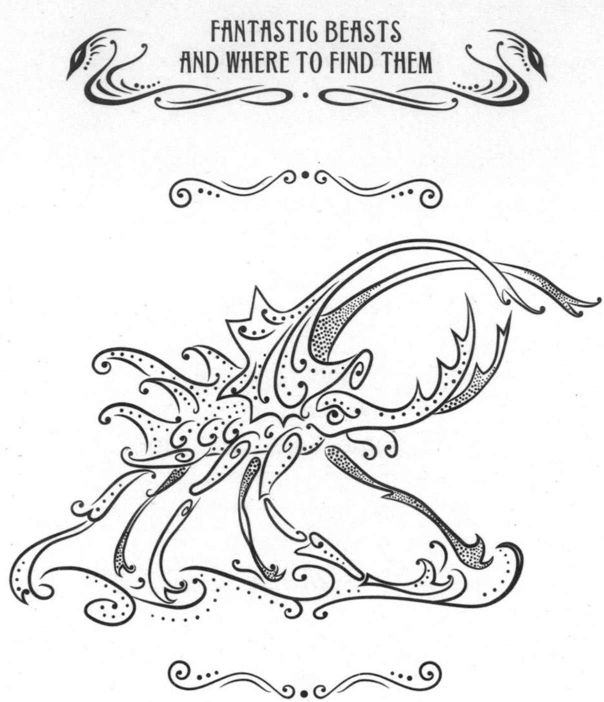

SCENE 62
INT. SECOND SALEM CHURCH, MAIN HALL—DAY— MONTAGE

MODESTY *approaches the long table at which many orphan children sit hungrily eating.*

MODESTY
(continuing her chant)
. . . my momma, your momma,
flying on a switch,
My momma, your momma,
witches never cry,

My momma, your momma,
witches gonna die!

MODESTY *gathers several of the children's leaflets from the table.*

MODESTY
Witch number one, drown in
a river!
Witch number two, gotta
noose to give her!
Witch number three . . .

TIME CUT:

The children, having finished their meal, leave the table with their leaflets and head for the door.

CHASTITY
(calling after them)
Hand out your leaflets! I'll
know if you dump 'em.
Tell me if you see anything
suspicious.

CLOSE ON CREDENCE *– he's washing dishes, but watching the children intently.*

MODESTY *follows the last of the children out of the church.*

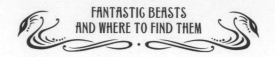

<u>SCENE 63</u>
EXT. STREET OUTSIDE SECOND SALEM CHURCH—DAY

MODESTY *stands in the middle of the busy street. She throws her leaflets high into the air, watching with glee as they fall around her.*

<u>SCENE 64</u>
INT. MACUSA CELL/CORRIDOR—DAY

Two EXECUTIONERS *in white coats lead a shackled* NEWT *and* TINA *down to a dark basement, away from the cell.*

NEWT *turns to look back.*

NEWT
(over his shoulder)
It was good to make your acquaintance, Jacob, and I hope you get your bakery.

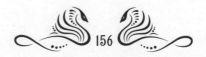

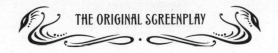

ANGLE ON JACOB, *scared, left behind, clutching at the bars of the cell. He waves forlornly after* NEWT.

SCENE 65
INT. INTERROGATION ROOM—DAY

A small, bare room, black-walled and windowless.

GRAVES *sits opposite* NEWT *at an interrogation desk, a file open in front of him.* NEWT *squints forward, a bright light shining into his eyes.*

TINA *stands behind, flanked by the two* EXECUTIONERS.

GRAVES
You're an interesting man,
Mr Scamander.

TINA
(stepping forwards)
Mr Graves—

GRAVES *holds a finger to his lips, signalling for* TINA *to be silent. The gesture is patronising, but authoritative.* TINA *looks kowtowed – she obeys, stepping back into the shadows.*

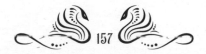

GRAVES *examines the file on his desk.*

GRAVES
You were thrown out of
Hogwarts for endangering
human life—

NEWT
That was an accident!

GRAVES
—with a beast. Yet one of
your teachers argued strongly
against your expulsion.
Now, what makes Albus
Dumbledore so fond of you?

NEWT
I really couldn't say.

GRAVES
So setting a pack of
dangerous creatures loose
here was just another
accident, is that right?

NEWT
Why would I do it
deliberately?

GRAVES

To expose wizardkind. To provoke war between the magical and non-magical worlds.

NEWT

Mass slaughter for the greater good, you mean?

GRAVES

Yes. Quite.

NEWT

I'm not one of Grindelwald's fanatics, Mr Graves.

A tiny change of expression tells us that NEWT *has scored a hit.* GRAVES *is looking more menacing.*

GRAVES

I wonder what you can tell me about this, Mr Scamander?

With a slow move of his hand, GRAVES *raises up the Obscurus from* NEWT'S *case. He brings it onto the desk – it is pulsing, swirling and hissing.*

CLOSE ON TINA *as she stares, disbelieving.*

GRAVES *reaches a hand towards the Obscurus – he's utterly fascinated. At his sudden close proximity, the Obscurus swirls faster, bubbling and shrinking backwards.*

NEWT *turns instinctively to* TINA. *Without fully realising why, it is she whom he wants to convince.*

NEWT
It's an Obscurus—
(off her look)
But, it's not what you think. I managed to separate it from the Sudanese girl as I tried to save her – I wanted to take it home, to study it—
(off TINA'S *shock)*
But it cannot survive outside that box, it could not hurt anyone, Tina!

GRAVES
So it's useless without the host?

NEWT
'Useless? Useless?' That is a parasitical magical force that killed a child. What on earth would you use it for?

NEWT, *anger finally boiling within him, stares at* GRAVES. TINA, *reacting to the atmosphere, also looks to* GRAVES – *concern and trepidation written across her face.*

GRAVES *stands, brushing off the questions, turning the blame back onto* NEWT.

GRAVES
You fool nobody, Mr Scamander. You brought this Obscurus into the city of New York in the hope of causing mass disruption, breaking the Statute of Secrecy and revealing the magical world—

NEWT
You know that can't hurt anyone, you know that!

GRAVES
—you are therefore guilty of a treasonous betrayal of your fellow wizards and are sentenced to death. Miss Goldstein, who has aided and abetted you—

NEWT

No, she's done nothing of the kind—

GRAVES

—she receives the same sentence.

The two EXECUTIONERS *step forwards. They calmly, intrusively, press the tips of their wands into* NEWT *and* TINA'S *necks.*

TINA *is so overcome with shock and fear that she can barely speak.*

GRAVES

(to the EXECUTIONERS*)*

Just do it immediately. I will inform President Picquery myself.

NEWT

Tina.

GRAVES *again places a finger to his lips.*

GRAVES

Shhhh.

(waving to the EXECUTIONERS*)*

Please.

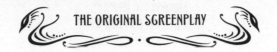

SCENE 66
INT. SHABBY BASEMENT MEETING ROOM— DAY

QUEENIE *is carrying a tray of coffee and mugs towards a meeting room.*

Suddenly she freezes, her eyes widen, a look of terror across her face. She drops the tray – cups smashing on the floor.

An assortment of low-level MACUSA functionaries turn to stare at her. QUEENIE *stares back, stunned, before running away down the corridor.*

SCENE 67
INT. CORRIDOR LEADING TO DEATH CELL— DAY

A long black metallic corridor leads into a pure white cell, which consists of a chair suspended magically over a square pool of rippling potion.

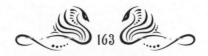

NEWT *and* TINA *are forced into this room by the* EXECUTIONERS. *A guard stands at the door.*

TINA
(*to* EXECUTIONER 1)
Don't do this – Bernadette – please—

EXECUTIONER 1
It don't hurt.

TINA *is led to the edge of the pool. She begins panicking, her breathing heavy and erratic.*

The smiling EXECUTIONER 1 *raises a wand and carefully extracts* TINA'S *happy memories from her head.* TINA *instantly calms – her expression now vacant, other-worldly.*

EXECUTIONER 1 *casts the memories into the potion, which ripples, coming alive with scenes from* TINA'S *life.*

A young TINA *smiles up as her mother calls.*

TINA'S MOTHER (*V.O.*)
Tina . . . Tina . . . come on, pumpkin – time for bed. Are you ready?

TINA
Momma . . .

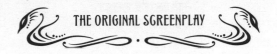

TINA'S MOTHER *appears in the pool, her expression loving and warm. The real* TINA *watches, smiling down.*

EXECUTIONER 1

Don't that look good. You wanna get in? Huh?

TINA *nods vacantly.*

SCENE 68
INT. MACUSA LOBBY—DAY

QUEENIE *stands in the crowded lobby. The elevator doors sound.*

ANGLE ON the elevator doors, which open revealing JACOB, *escorted by* SAM, *the Obliviator.*

QUEENIE *hurries towards them, determined.*

QUEENIE

Hey, Sam!

SAM

Hey, Queenie.

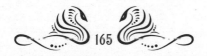

QUEENIE
They need you downstairs.
I'll Obliviate this guy.

SAM
You ain't qualified.

Grim-faced, QUEENIE *reads his mind.*

QUEENIE
Hey, Sam – does Cecily know
you been seeing Ruby?

ANGLE ON RUBY, *a MACUSA witch, standing ahead of them. She smiles at* SAM.

ANGLE ON QUEENIE *and* SAM – SAM *looks nervous.*

SAM
(appalled)
How'd you—?

QUEENIE
Let me Obliviate this guy
and she'll never hear about it
from me.

Stunned, SAM *backs away.* QUEENIE *seizes* JACOB'S *arm and marches him off across the cavernous lobby.*

JACOB
What are you doin'?

QUEENIE
Shhhh! Teen's in trouble, I'm trying to listen—
(*she reads* TINA'S *mind*)
Jacob, where's Newt's case?

JACOB
I think that guy Graves took it—

QUEENIE
Okay, come on—

JACOB
What? You're not gonna Obliviate me?

QUEENIE
Of course not – you're one of us now!

QUEENIE *hurries him towards the main staircase.*

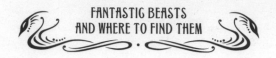

SCENE 69
INT. DEATH CELL—DAY

TINA *sits in the execution chair. She gazes down: beneath her swirl happy images of her family, her parents, a young* QUEENIE.

MEMORY:

We move into the pool and follow one of TINA'S *memories:* TINA *walks inside the Second Salem Church and up the stairs. She finds* MARY LOU, *standing over* CREDENCE, *belt in hand* – CREDENCE *looks terrified. In anger,* TINA *casts a spell, striking* MARY LOU. TINA *moves forward to comfort* CREDENCE.

TINA
It's okay.

ANGLE BACK ON real TINA, *still gazing into the pool, smiling wistfully.*

ANGLE ON NEWT, *who glances quickly down his own arm* – PICKETT *is clambering, quiet and agile, towards the shackles holding* NEWT'S *hands.*

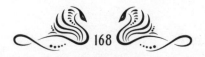

SCENE 70
INT. CORRIDOR LEADING TO GRAVES'S OFFICE—DAY

ANGLE ON the door to GRAVES'S *office.*

QUEENIE (*O.S.*)
Alohomora.

We see QUEENIE *and* JACOB *standing awkwardly outside* GRAVES'S *office,* QUEENIE *trying desperately to open the door.*

QUEENIE
Aberto . . .

The door remains locked.

QUEENIE
(*frustrated*)
Ugh. He would know a fancy spell to lock his office.

SCENE 71
INT. DEATH CELL—DAY

Back to PICKETT *as he finishes unlocking the shackles holding* NEWT'S *wrists, and quickly climbs onto* EXECUTIONER 2'S *coat.*

EXECUTIONER 2
(*to* NEWT)
Okay, let's get the good stuff out of you—

EXECUTIONER 2 *raises her wand to* NEWT'S *forehead.* NEWT *seizes his opportunity – he jumps backwards out of the way before revealing the Swooping Evil, which he throws forwards towards the pool. He then swiftly turns and punches the guard, knocking him out cold.*

The Swooping Evil has now expanded into a gigantic, spooky but weirdly beautiful butterfly-esque reptile with skeletal wings. It continues to circle round and round the pool.

PICKETT *clambers onto* EXECUTIONER 2'S *arm and bites, startling and distracting her, giving* NEWT *time to grab her arms and take aim with her wand. A spell fires, hitting* EXECUTIONER 1, *who drops to the floor, her wand falling into the pool. As it falls, the liquid rises up in viscous black bubbles, instantly engulfing the wand.*

In reaction, TINA'S *memories turn from good to bad: we see* MARY LOU, *pointing aggressively at* TINA.

MARY LOU

Witch!

TINA, *still enraptured by the pool, looks increasingly terrified. Her chair is lowering closer and closer to the liquid.*

The Swooping Evil glides across the room, knocking EXECUTIONER 2 *to the ground.*

<u>SCENE 72</u>

INT. CORRIDOR LEADING TO GRAVES'S OFFICE—DAY

After a quick glance around, JACOB *gives the door a hefty kick. It breaks open.* JACOB *stands guard as* QUEENIE *runs in and grabs* NEWT'S *case and* TINA'S *wand.*

<u>SCENE 73</u>
INT. DEATH CELL—DAY

TINA *snaps out of her reverie and screams.*

TINA
MR SCAMANDER!

The liquid has now turned into a black bubbling death potion. It rises up, surrounding TINA *on her chair.* TINA *stands up to get away, almost falling off in her haste. She tries desperately to regain her balance.*

NEWT
Don't panic!

TINA
What do you suggest I do instead?

NEWT *makes a strange tutting sound, commanding the Swooping Evil to circle the pool once more.*

NEWT
Jump . . .

TINA *looks at the Swooping Evil – fearful, disbelieving.*

TINA
Are you crazy?

NEWT

Jump on him.

NEWT *stands on the edge of the pool watching the Swooping Evil as it circles round and round* TINA.

NEWT

Tina, listen to me. I'll catch you. Tina!

The two make intense eye contact, NEWT *trying to reassure …*

The liquid has now risen up in waves to TINA'S *full height – she's losing sight of* NEWT.

NEWT

(insistent, very calm)

I'll catch you. I've got you Tina …

Suddenly NEWT *cries out.*

NEWT

Go!

TINA *jumps in between two of the waves, just as the Swooping Evil passes. She lands on its back, only inches away from the swirling liquid, then hops quickly forwards, straight into* NEWT'S *open arms.*

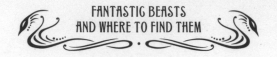

For a split second NEWT *and* TINA *gaze at each other, before* NEWT *raises his hand, recalling the Swooping Evil, which folds into a cocoon once more.*

NEWT *grabs* TINA'S *hand and heads for the exit.*

NEWT

Come on!

SCENE 74
INT. DEATH CELL CORRIDOR—DAY

QUEENIE *and* JACOB *march along the corridor with purpose.*

An alarm goes off in the distance – other wizards hurry past them in the opposite direction.

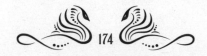

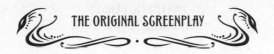

SCENE 75
INT. MACUSA LOBBY—MINUTES LATER—DAY

The alarm blares out across the lobby.

Confusion reigns among the crowd – people gather in groups, nervously chattering, others scurry about, urgent, anxious.

A team of Aurors hurtles across the lobby, headed directly for the stairs leading down to the basement.

SCENE 76
INT. DEATH CELL CORRIDOR/BASEMENT CORRIDOR—DAY

NEWT *and* TINA, *hand in hand, charge through the basement corridors. Suddenly accosted by the group of Aurors, they turn, darting behind pillars, just missing the fired curses and spells.*

NEWT *again sends out the Swooping Evil, which swirls overhead, flying in and out of pillars, blocking curses and knocking Aurors to the ground.*

ANGLE ON the Swooping Evil using its proboscis to probe in one of the Auror's ears.

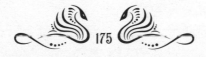

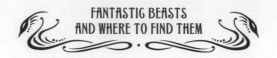

NEWT
(making a clicking sound)
LEAVE HIS BRAINS. Come on! Come on!

TINA *and* NEWT *run onwards, the Swooping Evil flying after, blocking curses as it goes.*

TINA
What *is* that thing?

NEWT
Swooping Evil.

TINA
Well, I love it!

ANGLE ON QUEENIE *and* JACOB, *walking briskly through the basement.* NEWT *and* TINA *sprint round the corner and almost collide with them. The four stare at one another, panic on all their faces.*

Finally QUEENIE *gestures to the case.*

QUEENIE
Get in!

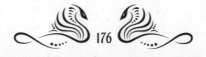

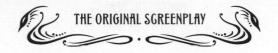

SCENE 77
INT. STAIRS LEADING TO CELLS—MOMENTS LATER—DAY

GRAVES *moves down the stairs with urgency. For the first time, a look of panic on his face.*

SCENE 78
INT. MACUSA LOBBY—MINUTES LATER—DAY

QUEENIE *moves quickly across the lobby floor, trying desperately not to be conspicuous in her haste, but acutely aware of the need to leave. A flustered* ABERNATHY *emerges from a crowd of wizards.*

ABERNATHY

Queenie!

QUEENIE, *poised at the top of the stairs, turns and composes herself.* ABERNATHY *moves towards her, straightening his tie, trying to appear calm and authoritative –* QUEENIE *obviously makes him nervous.*

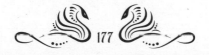

ABERNATHY
(a large smile)
Where you going?

QUEENIE *puts on an alluringly innocent expression and holds the case behind her back.*

QUEENIE
I'm . . . I'm sick, Mr Abernathy.

She coughs a little, widening her eyes.

ABERNATHY
Again? Well – what've you got there?

A beat.

QUEENIE *thinks fast, her face quickly breaking into a breathtaking smile.*

QUEENIE
Ladies' things.

QUEENIE *produces the case and innocently trots up the steps towards* ABERNATHY.

QUEENIE
You wanna take a look? I don't mind.

ABERNATHY *is overcome with embarrassment.*

ABERNATHY
(swallowing hard)
Oh! Good gravy, no! I – you get well now!

QUEENIE
(smiling sweetly and arranging his tie)
Thanks!

QUEENIE *immediately turns and hurries down the stairs leaving* ABERNATHY – *heart racing – staring after her.*

SCENE 79
EXT. STREETS OF NEW YORK—LATE AFTERNOON

HIGH WIDE above New York. We zoom over rooftops before diving down through streets and alleyways, past speeding cars and cackling children.

We come to rest in an alleyway at the Second Salem Church, where CREDENCE *is pasting up posters advertising* MARY LOU'S *next meeting.*

GRAVES *Apparates in the alleyway.* CREDENCE, *startled, backs away, but* GRAVES *makes straight for him, his tone and manner urgent, forceful.*

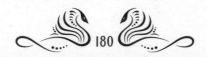

GRAVES
Credence. Have you found the child?

CREDENCE
I can't.

GRAVES, *impatient but feigning calm, holds out his hand – suddenly seeming caring, affectionate.*

GRAVES
Show me.

CREDENCE *whimpers and cowers, almost backing further away.* GRAVES *gently takes* CREDENCE'S *hand in his own and examines it – the hand is covered in deep red cuts, sore and bleeding.*

GRAVES
Shhhh. My boy, the sooner we find this child, the sooner you can put that pain in the past where it belongs.

GRAVES *gently, almost seductively, moves his thumb across the cuts, healing them instantly.* CREDENCE *stares.*

GRAVES *seems to make a decision. He puts on an earnest, trustworthy expression as, from his pocket, he produces a chain bearing the symbol of the Deathly Hallows.*

GRAVES
I want you to have this, Credence. I would trust very few with it—

GRAVES *moves close, placing the chain around* CREDENCE'S *neck as he whispers.*

GRAVES
Very few.

GRAVES *places his hands on either side of* CREDENCE'S *neck, drawing him in, his speech quiet, intimate.*

GRAVES
... but you – you're different.

CREDENCE *is unsure, both nervous of and attracted by* GRAVES'S *behaviour.*

GRAVES *rests his hand on* CREDENCE'S *heart, covering the pendant.*

GRAVES
Now, when you find the child, touch this symbol and I will know, and I will come to you.

GRAVES *moves even closer to* CREDENCE, *his face*

inches from the boy's neck – the effect is both alluring and threatening – as he whispers.

GRAVES
Do this and you will be honoured among wizards. For ever.

GRAVES *pulls* CREDENCE *into a hug which, with his hand on* CREDENCE'S *neck, seems more controlling than affectionate.* CREDENCE, *overwhelmed by the seeming affection, closes his eyes and relaxes slightly.*

GRAVES *slowly backs away, stroking* CREDENCE'S *neck.* CREDENCE *keeps his eyes closed, longing for the human contact to continue.*

GRAVES
(whispers)
The child is dying, Credence. Time is running out.

Abruptly, GRAVES *strides back down the alleyway and Disapparates.*

SCENE 80
EXT. ROOFTOP WITH PIGEON COOP—DUSK

A rooftop overlooking the whole city. In the middle sits a small wooden shed, which houses a pigeon coop.

NEWT *steps up onto a ledge and stands looking over the immense city.* PICKETT *sits on his shoulder, clicking.*

JACOB *is inside the shed, looking at the pigeon coop as* QUEENIE *enters.*

QUEENIE
Your grandfather kept pigeons? Mine bred owls. I used to love feeding 'em.

ANGLE ON NEWT *and* TINA – TINA *has joined* NEWT *in standing on the ledge.*

TINA
Graves always insisted the disturbances were caused by a beast. We need to catch all your creatures, so he can't keep using them as a scapegoat.

NEWT
There's only one still missing. Dougal, my Demiguise.

TINA

Dougal?

NEWT

Slight problem is that … um, he's invisible.

TINA

(this is so ridiculous that she can't help but smile)

Invisible?

NEWT

Yes – most of the time … he does … um …

TINA

How do you catch something that—

NEWT

(beginning to smile)

With immense difficulty.

TINA

Oh …

They smile at each other – there's a new warmth between them, NEWT *still awkward but somehow unable to stop staring at* TINA *as she smiles.*

TINA *moves slowly towards* NEWT.

A beat.

TINA

Gnarlak!

NEWT

(taken aback)

Excuse me?

TINA

(conspiratorial, excited)

Gnarlak – he was an informant of mine when I was an Auror! He used to trade in magical creatures on the side—

NEWT

He wouldn't happen to have an interest in paw prints would he?

TINA

He's interested in anything he can sell.

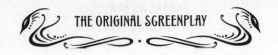

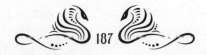

SCENE 81
EXT. THE BLIND PIG—NIGHT

TINA *leads the group down an insalubrious back alley covered in bins, crates and discarded objects. She locates a set of steps leading to a basement apartment and motions them down.*

The steps appear to lead to a dead end: the doorway has been bricked up. Instead, a poster of a simpering debutante in evening dress, gazing at herself in a mirror, covers the end of the walkway.

TINA *and* QUEENIE *stand in front of this poster. They turn to each other and, in unison, raise their wands. As they do so, their work clothes transform into stunning flapper party dresses.* TINA *looks up at* NEWT, *somewhat embarrassed by her new attire.* QUEENIE *gazes at* JACOB, *a cheeky smile on her face.*

TINA *steps towards the poster and slowly raises her hand. As she does so, the eyes of the debutante move upwards, following her every move.* TINA *knocks slowly on the door four times.*

NEWT, *sensing the need for a change, hastily magics himself a small bow tie.* JACOB *looks on, jealously.*

A hatch opens: the painted eyes of the debutante whip back to reveal the gaze of a suspicious guard.

<u>SCENE 82</u>
INT. THE BLIND PIG—NIGHT

A seedy, low-ceilinged speakeasy for the down and out of New York's magical community. Every witch and wizard criminal in New York is here, their wanted posters hanging proudly on the walls. A glimpse of 'GELLERT

GRINDELWALD: WANTED FOR NO-MAJ SLAYINGS IN EUROPE'.

A glamorous goblin JAZZ SINGER *croons on a stage full of goblin musicians, smoky images wafting from her wand to illustrate her lyrics. All is dingy and shabby, an atmosphere of menacing fun.*

JAZZ SINGER

The phoenix cried fat tears of
  pearl,
When the dragon snapped up
  his best girl,
And the Billywig forgot to
  twirl,
When his sweetheart left him
  cold,
And the unicorn done lost his
  horn,
And the Hippogriff feels all
  forlorn,
'Cause their lady loves have
  upped and gawn,
Or that's what I've been
  told—

JACOB *stands at the seemingly unmanned bar, waiting to be served.*

JACOB
How do I get a drink in this joint?

Out of nowhere, a thin bottle of brown liquid zooms towards him. He catches it, stunned.

The head of a HOUSE-ELF *peers up at him from behind the bar.*

HOUSE-ELF
What? Ain't you ever seen a house-elf before?

JACOB
Oh, no, yeah, no, yeah of course I have ... I love house-elves.

JACOB *tries to act nonchalant – he removes the cork from the bottle.*

JACOB
My uncle's a house-elf.

The HOUSE-ELF *– not fooled – raises himself up, leaning on the bar to stare at* JACOB.

QUEENIE *approaches. She looks downcast as she orders.*

QUEENIE
Six shots of gigglewater and a lobe blaster, please.

The HOUSE-ELF *reluctantly shuffles off to fulfil her request.* JACOB *and* QUEENIE *look at each other.* JACOB *reaches out and takes one of the gigglewater shots.*

QUEENIE
Are all No-Majs like you?

JACOB
(trying to be serious, almost seductive)
No, I'm the only one like me.

Maintaining strong eye contact with QUEENIE, JACOB *knocks back the shot. Suddenly he emits a raucous, high-pitched giggle.* QUEENIE *laughs sweetly at his look of surprise.*

ANGLE ON a HOUSE-ELF *serving a drink to a giant, whose hand dwarfs the mug he is handed.*

ANGLE ON NEWT *and* TINA *sitting at a table alone. There's an awkward silence.* NEWT *studies the characters in the room: hooded and heavily scarred witches and wizards gamble magical artefacts in a game with runic dice.*

TINA
(looking around)
I've arrested half of the people in here.

NEWT
You can tell me to mind my own business ... but I saw something in that death potion back there. I saw you – hugging – that Second Salem boy.

TINA
His name's Credence. His mother beats him. She beats all those kids she adopted, but she seems to hate him the most.

NEWT
(realising)
And she was the No-Maj you attacked?

TINA
That's how I lost my job. I went for her in front of a meeting of her crazy followers – they all had to

be Obliviated. It was a big
scandal.

QUEENIE *signals from across the room.*

QUEENIE
(whispers)
It's him.

GNARLAK *has emerged from the depths of the speakeasy. Smoking a cigar and smartly dressed, for a goblin, he has a sly, smooth demeanour like a mafia boss. He eyes the newcomers as he walks.*

JAZZ SINGER (*O.S.*)
Yes, love has set the beasts astir,
The dang'rous and the meek
concur,
It's ruffled feathers, fleece and
fur,
'Cause love drives all of us
wild.

GNARLAK *sits himself at the end of their table, an air of confidence and dangerous control. A* HOUSE-ELF *hastily brings him a drink.*

GNARLAK
So – you're the guy with the
case full of monsters, huh?

NEWT

News travels fast. I was hoping you'd be able to tell me if there have been any sightings. Tracks. That sort of thing.

GNARLAK *downs his drink. Another* HOUSE-ELF *brings him a document to sign.*

GNARLAK

You've got a big price on your head, Mr Scamander. Why should I help you instead of turnin' you in?

NEWT

I take it I'll have to make it worth your while?

The HOUSE-ELF *scurries off holding the signed document.*

GNARLAK

Hmm – let's consider it a cover charge.

NEWT *pulls out a couple of Galleons and slides them across the table towards* GNARLAK, *who barely looks up.*

GNARLAK
(not impressed)
Huh – MACUSA's offerin' more'n that.

A beat.

NEWT *pulls out a beautiful metal instrument and places it on the table.*

GNARLAK
Lunascope? I got five.

NEWT *rummages in his coat pocket and pulls out a glowing, frozen ruby egg instead.*

NEWT
Frozen Ashwinder egg.

GNARLAK
(finally interested)
You see – now we're—

GNARLAK *suddenly spots* PICKETT, *who is peeking out of* NEWT'S *pocket.*

GNARLAK
—wait a minute – that's a Bowtruckle, right?

PICKETT *quickly retreats and* NEWT *puts a hand protectively over his pocket.*

NEWT

No.

GNARLAK

Ah, come on, that's a Bowtruckle – they pick locks – am I right?

NEWT

You're not having him.

GNARLAK

Well, good luck gettin' back alive, Mr Scamander, what with the whole of MACUSA on your back.

GNARLAK *gets up and walks away.*

NEWT

(in agony)

All right.

GNARLAK, *turned away from* NEWT, *smiles viciously.*

NEWT *extracts* PICKETT *from his pocket.* PICKETT *clings to* NEWT'S *hands, madly clicking and whining.*

NEWT

Pickett …

NEWT *slowly hands* PICKETT *over to* GNARLAK. PICKETT *reaches his little arms forward, imploring* NEWT *to take him back.* NEWT *cannot look at him.*

GNARLAK

Ah, yeah …

(*to* NEWT)

Somethin' invisible's been wreakin' havoc around Fifth Avenue. You may wanna check out Macy's department store. Might help what you're looking for.

NEWT

(*sotto voce*)

Dougal …

(*to* GNARLAK)

Right, one last thing. There's a Mr Graves who works at MACUSA – I was wondering what you knew of his background.

GNARLAK *stares. A sense that there is much that he could say – and that he'd rather die than say it.*

GNARLAK
You ask a lot of questions, Mr Scamander. That can get you killed.

ANGLE ON a HOUSE-ELF *carrying a crate of bottles.*

HOUSE-ELF
MACUSA ARE COMING!

The HOUSE-ELF *Disapparates. Other customers throughout the bar hurriedly do the same.*

TINA
(getting to her feet)
You tipped them off!

GNARLAK *stares at them, chuckling menacingly.*

Behind QUEENIE, *the wanted posters on the wall update to show* NEWT *and* TINA'S *faces.*

Aurors begin Apparating into the speakeasy.

JACOB, *seemingly innocent, saunters up to* GNARLAK.

JACOB
Sorry, Mr Gnarlak—

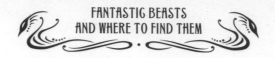

JACOB *punches* GNARLAK *straight in the face, knocking him backwards.* QUEENIE *looks delighted.*

JACOB
– reminds me of my foreman!

Throughout the bar, various customers are being apprehended by the Aurors.

NEWT *scrambles about on the floor looking for* PICKETT. *Around him people are running, diving away from Aurors, trying to escape the bar.* NEWT *finally finds* PICKETT *on a table leg, grabs him and runs towards his group.*

JACOB *grabs another shot of gigglewater and knocks it back. He giggles uproariously as* NEWT *grabs his elbow and the group Disapparates.*

SCENE 83
INT. SECOND SALEM CHURCH—NIGHT

The long room is dimly lit by one set of lights. There's barely any noise.

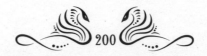

CHASTITY *sits primly at the long table in the middle of the*

church. She formulaically arranges leaflets and places them in little bags.

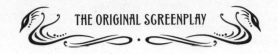

MODESTY *sits opposite in a nightdress, reading a book. In the deep background,* MARY LOU *busies herself in her bedroom.*

MODESTY *is the only one to register a small clunk from upstairs.*

SCENE 84
INT. MODESTY'S BEDROOM—NIGHT

A bleak room. A single bed, an oil-lamp, a sampler on the wall: An Alphabet of Sin. MODESTY'S *dolls lined up on a shelf. One with a little noose around its neck, another tied to a stake.*

CREDENCE *scrabbles to get underneath* MODESTY'S *bed. He looks among the boxes and objects hidden there, then suddenly stops, staring . . .*

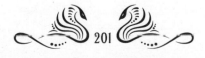

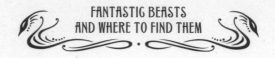

SCENE 85

INT. SECOND SALEM CHURCH—NIGHT

MODESTY *stands at the bottom of the stairs, looking up. She slowly ascends.*

SCENE 86

INT. MODESTY'S BEDROOM—NIGHT

ANGLE ON CREDENCE'S *face under the bed –* CREDENCE *has found a toy wand. He stares, unable to draw his eyes from it.*

Behind him, MODESTY *enters.*

MODESTY
Whatchoo doin', Credence?

CREDENCE *bangs his head on the bed in his haste to get out. He emerges, dusty and scared. He is relieved to see that it is only* MODESTY *but she, on seeing the wand, is terrified.*

CREDENCE
Where'd you get this?

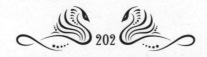

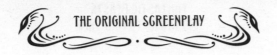

MODESTY
(frightened whisper)
Give it back, Credence. It's just a toy!

The door bangs open. MARY LOU *enters. Her gaze travels from* MODESTY *to* CREDENCE *and the toy wand – she is angrier than we have ever seen her.*

MARY LOU
(to CREDENCE*)*
What is this?

SCENE 87
INT. SECOND SALEM CHURCH—NIGHT

HOLD ON CHASTITY, *still filling bags with leaflets.*

MARY LOU (*O.S.*)
Take it off!

CHASTITY *glances up towards the landing.*

SCENE 88

INT. SECOND SALEM CHURCH, UPSTAIRS LANDING—NIGHT

MARY LOU *stands on the landing overlooking the main church below. Seen from below her figure is powerful, almost deified.*

MARY LOU *turns back towards* CREDENCE *and slowly, her face full of loathing, snaps the wand in two.*

As MODESTY *cowers,* CREDENCE *begins to remove his belt.* MARY LOU *holds out her hand and takes it.*

CREDENCE
(pleading)
Ma . . .

MARY LOU
I am not your ma! Your mother was a wicked, unnatural woman!

MODESTY *forces her way between them.*

MODESTY
It was mine.

MARY LOU
Modesty—

Suddenly the belt is whipped out of MARY LOU'S *hands by supernatural means and falls like a dead snake in a far corner.* MARY LOU *looks at her hand – it is cut and bleeding from the force of the movement.*

MARY LOU *is stunned – she glances between* MODESTY *and* CREDENCE.

MARY LOU
(frightened but covering it)
What is this?

MODESTY *stares defiantly directly back at her. In the background we see* CREDENCE *crouched down, hugging his knees and shaking.*

Trying to remain composed, MARY LOU *moves slowly to retrieve the belt. Before she can touch it, the belt slithers away across the floor.*

MARY LOU *backs away, tears of fear welling in her eyes. She turns slowly back towards the children.*

As she moves, an almighty force explodes into her: a bestial, screeching, dark mass that consumes her. Her scream is blood-curdling as the force throws her backwards, striking a wooden beam, flinging her over the balcony.

MARY LOU *smashes down onto the floor of the main church, her body lifeless, her face bearing the same scars seen on the face of* SENATOR SHAW.

The Dark force flies through the church, upending the table and destroying everything in sight.

SCENE 89
EXT. DEPARTMENT STORE—NIGHT

WIDE SHOT of a department store, its windows full of glamorously dressed mannequins.

JACOB *approaches the shop windows staring at a handbag which, seemingly of its own accord, is sliding down the arm of a mannequin.* NEWT, TINA *and* QUEENIE *hurry up behind him and watch as the bag hovers in mid-air and floats off into the store.*

SCENE 90

INT. DEPARTMENT STORE—NIGHT

A well-presented department store decorated for Christmas, with aisles full of expensive jewellery, shoes, hats and perfume. The place is shut down for the night, all the lights are off, no noises can be heard.

We see the handbag float down the central aisle, accompanied by small grunting noises.

NEWT *and the group quickly tiptoe through the store, coming to hide behind a large plastic Christmas display. They eye up the floating handbag.*

NEWT
(whispers)
So Demiguises are fundamentally peaceful, but they can give a nasty nip if provoked.

The Demiguise itself appears – a silvery-haired, orangutan-like creature, with a curious, wizened face – clambering over a display to reach a box of sweets.

NEWT
(to JACOB *and* QUEENIE*)*
You two . . . head that way.

They start moving.

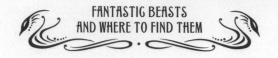

NEWT
And try very hard not to be predictable.

JACOB *and* QUEENIE *exchange perplexed glances before heading off.*

A small roar can be heard in the distance.

ANGLE ON the Demiguise which, on hearing the sound, looks up towards the ceiling, before continuing to gather sweets, now shovelling them into its handbag.

TINA *(O.S.)*
Was that the Demiguise?

NEWT
No, I think it might be the reason that the Demiguise is here.

ANGLE ON NEWT *and* TINA*, moving swiftly down an aisle towards the Demiguise, which is now moving away through the store.*

Realising it's been spotted, the Demiguise turns and looks at NEWT *quizzically, before moving up a set of side stairs.* NEWT *smiles and moves to follow.*

SCENE 91

INT. DEPARTMENT STORE, ATTIC STOREROOM—NIGHT

A huge, dark attic-space, filled floor to ceiling with shelves packed with boxes of china: dinner services, teacups and general kitchenware.

The Demiguise walks along the attic in a patch of moonlight. It glances around before stopping and emptying its handbag full of confectionery.

NEWT (*O.S.*)

Its sight operates on probability, so it can foresee the most likely immediate future.

NEWT *comes into view, creeping up behind the Demiguise.*

TINA (*O.S.*)

So what's it doing?

NEWT

It's babysitting.

The Demiguise holds up one of the sweets, seeming to offer it up to someone or something.

TINA

What did you just say—?

NEWT
(calm and whispering)
This is my fault. I thought
I had them all – but I must
have miscounted.

JACOB *and* QUEENIE *enter quietly.* NEWT *moves calmly forwards and kneels beside the Demiguise, which makes space for him in front of the sweets.* NEWT *carefully places his case down.*

ANGLE ON TINA, *a shift of light reveals the scales of a large creature hiding in the rafters of the attic.* TINA *looks up in horror.*

TINA
It was babysitting that?

ANGLE ON the ceiling as the face of an Occamy comes into view – just like the small blue snake-like birds seen in the case, this Occamy is huge, coiled round and round itself to fill the entire attic roof-space.

The Occamy moves slowly down towards NEWT *and the Demiguise who, again, offers up a sweet.* NEWT *remains very still.*

NEWT
Occamies are choranaptyxic.
So they – grow – to fill –
available – space.

The Occamy spots NEWT, *and cranes its head towards him.* NEWT *holds up a hand, gently.*

NEWT

Mummy's here.

ANGLE ON the Demiguise, whose eyes flash a brilliant blue – a sign that it's having a premonition.

FLASHCUTS:

A Christmas bauble rolls across the floor; the Occamy is panicking, NEWT *clasping its back, being flung about the room; the Demiguise is suddenly on* JACOB'S *back.*

BACK TO the Demiguise as its eyes turn back to brown.

QUEENIE *moves slowly forward, staring at the Occamy. As she does so she accidentally kicks a tiny glass bauble on the floor, which jingles as it rolls. At the sound, the Occamy rears up, screeching.* NEWT *tries to calm the large creature.*

NEWT

Woah! Woah!

JACOB *and* QUEENIE *stagger backwards to find cover. The Demiguise runs away and jumps into* JACOB'S *arms.*

The Occamy swoops, scooping NEWT *up onto its back as it violently thrashes about the attic, sending shelves flying.* NEWT *shouts out.*

NEWT
Right, we need an insect, any
kind of insect – and a teapot!
Find a teapot!

TINA *army-crawls through the chaos, dodging falling items, trying to find what* NEWT *has asked for.*

The wings of the Occamy crash down to the floor, narrowly missing JACOB *as he stumbles around, encumbered by the Demiguise now clinging to his back.*

NEWT *finds it harder and harder to hold on as the Occamy becomes more and more distressed, its wings now thrashing upwards, destroying the roof of the building.*

JACOB *turns, he and the Demiguise spotting a stray cockroach on a crate.* JACOB *reaches his hand up to grab it, when part of the Occamy crashes down, destroying the crate and his chance.*

ANGLE ON TINA, *crawling across the floor with great determination, in hot pursuit of a cockroach.*

ANGLE ON QUEENIE, *who screams as she's knocked to the floor by the force of the Occamy.* JACOB *runs up behind her and dives forwards, flat onto the floor, finally laying claim to a cockroach.* TINA *stands, clutching a teapot and screaming.*

TINA

Teapot!

At this noise, the Occamy rears its head once more, causing its tail to writhe, squashing and pinning JACOB *– with the Demiguise – against one of the rafters.*

JACOB *and* TINA *are now at opposite ends of the room, neither daring to move, swathes of Occamy scales between them.*

ANGLE ON JACOB *and the Demiguise – the Demiguise looks shiftily up to the side and promptly vanishes.* JACOB *slowly turns to follow the Demiguise's gaze – the Occamy's face is inches away from his own, staring with full intensity at the cockroach in his hand.* JACOB *barely dares to breathe.*

NEWT *peers round from behind the Occamy's head and whispers.*

NEWT

Roach in teapot . . .

JACOB *gulps, trying not to make eye contact with the huge creature next to him.*

JACOB

(trying to soothe the Occamy)

Shhhh!

JACOB *widens his eyes at* TINA, *warning her of his intent.*

IN SLOW MOTION:

JACOB *throws the roach. We watch it soar through the air as the Occamy's body begins to move once more, uncurling and swirling round the room.*

NEWT *jumps from the Occamy's back, landing safely on the floor, while* QUEENIE *takes cover, placing a colander over her head.*

TINA *runs, teapot outstretched, hurdling over the Occamy's coils as she goes – a heroic sight. She lands on her knees in the centre of the room, the cockroach falling perfectly into the teapot.*

The Occamy rears up, shrinking rapidly as it rises, before diving down head first. TINA *lowers her head, bracing herself for a hit. The Occamy races down towards the teapot, and glides seamlessly inside.*

NEWT *races forwards and jams a lid on top of the teapot. He and* TINA *breathe heavily: relief.*

NEWT
Choranaptyxic. They also *shrink* to fit the available space.

ANGLE INSIDE the teapot – the now tiny Occamy gobbling down its cockroach.

TINA
Tell me the truth – was that everything that came out of the case?

NEWT
That's everything – and that's the truth.

SCENE 92
INT. NEWT'S CASE—SHORTLY AFTERWARDS—NIGHT

JACOB *holds the Demiguise's hand, leading it through its enclosure.*

NEWT (*O.S.*)
Here she comes.

JACOB *lifts the Demiguise up and into its nest.*

JACOB
(to the Demiguise)
Happy to be home? Bet you're exhausted buddy. Come on – there you go – that's right.

TINA *is tentatively holding the baby Occamy. Supervised by* NEWT, *she places it gently into its nest.*

HOLD ON TINA *as she looks around at the Erumpent, now stamping through her enclosure.* TINA'S *face is full of wonder and admiration.* JACOB *chuckles at her expression.*

PICKETT *gives* NEWT *a sharp pinch from inside his pocket.*

NEWT
Ouch!

NEWT *fishes* PICKETT *out, holding him up on his hand as he walks through the various enclosures.*

We see the Niffler sitting in a small enclave, surrounded by its various treasures.

NEWT
Right ... I think we need to talk. See, I wouldn't have let him keep you, Pickett. Pick, I would rather chop off my

hand than get rid of you . . .
after everything you have
done for me – now come on.

NEWT *has reached* FRANK'S *area.*

NEWT
Pick – we've talked about
sulking before, haven't we?
Pickett – come on give me a
smile. Pickett, give me a . . .

PICKETT *sticks out his tiny tongue and blows a raspberry at* NEWT

NEWT
All right – now, that is
beneath you.

NEWT *places* PICKETT *on his shoulder and starts busying himself with various buckets of feed.*

ANGLE ON a photograph inside NEWT'S *shed, which shows a beautiful girl – the girl smiles suggestively.* QUEENIE *stares at the photo.*

QUEENIE
Hey, Newt. Who is she?

NEWT
Ah . . . that's no one.

QUEENIE
(reading his mind)
Leta Lestrange? I've heard of that family. Aren't they kinda – you know?

NEWT
Please don't read my mind.

A beat as QUEENIE *drinks the whole story out of* NEWT'S *head. She looks both intrigued and saddened.* NEWT *continues to work, trying hard to pretend* QUEENIE *isn't reading his mind.*

QUEENIE *steps forwards, closer to* NEWT.

NEWT
(angry, embarrassed)
Sorry, I asked you not to.

QUEENIE
I know, I'm sorry, I can't help it. People are easiest to read when they're hurting.

NEWT
I'm not hurting. Anyway, it was a long time ago.

QUEENIE
That was a real close friendship you had at school.

NEWT
(attempting to be dismissive)
Yes, well, neither of us really fitted in at school, so we—

QUEENIE
—became real close. For years.

In the background we see TINA, *who has noticed that* NEWT *and* QUEENIE *are talking.*

QUEENIE
(concerned)
She was a taker. You need a giver.

TINA *walks towards them.*

TINA
What are you two talking about?

NEWT
Ah nothing.

QUEENIE
School.

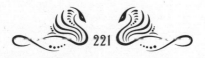

NEWT

School.

JACOB

(putting on his jacket)

Did you say school? Is there a school? A wizardry school here? In America?

QUEENIE

Of course – Ilvermorny! It's only the best wizard school in the whole world!

NEWT

I think you'll find the best wizarding school in the world is Hogwarts!

QUEENIE

HOGWASH.

A gigantic crack of thunder. The Thunderbird, FRANK, *rises into the air screeching, flapping his wings vigorously, his body turning black and gold, his eyes flashing lightning.*

NEWT *stands, examining the bird, concerned.*

NEWT

Danger. He senses danger.

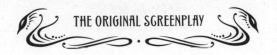

SCENE 93
EXT. SECOND SALEM CHURCH—NIGHT

GRAVES *Apparates in the shadows. Wand drawn, he slowly approaches the church, examining the scene of decimation. Rather than nervous, he seems intrigued, almost excited.*

SCENE 94
INT. SECOND SALEM CHURCH—NIGHT

The place is destroyed – moonlight filters through gaps in the roof, and CHASTITY *lies dead amid debris from the attack.*

GRAVES *slowly enters the church, wand still drawn. Eerie sobbing can be heard from somewhere in the building.*

MARY LOU'S *body lies on the floor in front of him – the marks on her face visible in the moonlight.* GRAVES *considers the corpse: a realisation dawning on his face – no horror, merely wariness and intense interest.*

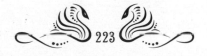

FOCUS ON CREDENCE, *cowering at the back of the church, whimpering and clutching his pendant of the Deathly Hallows.* GRAVES *steps quickly towards him, bends down, cradling* CREDENCE'S *head. However, there's little tenderness to his voice as he speaks.*

GRAVES
The Obscurial – was here?
Where did she go?

CREDENCE *looks up into* GRAVES'S *face – he is utterly traumatised and unable to explain – his face a plea for affection.*

CREDENCE
Help me. Help me.

GRAVES
Didn't you tell me you had
another sister?

CREDENCE *begins to weep again.* GRAVES *places a hand on his neck, his face contorting with stress as he tries to remain calm.*

CREDENCE
Please help me.

GRAVES
Where's your other sister,
Credence? The little one?
Where did she go?

CREDENCE *trembles and mumbles.*

CREDENCE
Please help me.

Suddenly vicious, GRAVES *slaps* CREDENCE *hard across the face.*

CREDENCE*, stunned, stares at* GRAVES.

GRAVES
Your sister's in grave danger.
We need to find her.

CREDENCE *is aghast, unable to comprehend that his hero has hit him.* GRAVES *grabs him and pulls him up onto his feet, as they Disapparate.*

SCENE 95
EXT. TENEMENT IN THE BRONX—NIGHT

A deserted street. GRAVES, *led by* CREDENCE, *approaches a tenement building.*

SCENE 96
INT. TENEMENT IN THE BRONX, HALLWAY—NIGHT

Inside, the building is miserable, dilapidated. CREDENCE *and* GRAVES *climb the stairwell.*

GRAVES (*O.S.*)
What is this place?

CREDENCE
Ma adopted Modesty out of here. From a family of twelve. She misses her brothers and sisters. She still talks about them.

GRAVES, *wand in hand, looks around the landing – there are numerous darkened doorways stretching out in several directions.*

CREDENCE, *still shell-shocked, has stopped in the stairwell.*

GRAVES
Where is she?

CREDENCE *looks down – at a loss.*

CREDENCE
I don't know.

GRAVES *becomes increasingly impatient – he's so close to his goal. He marches forward into one of the rooms.*

GRAVES
(contemptuous)
You're a Squib, Credence.
I could smell it off you the
minute I met you.

CREDENCE'S *face falls.*

CREDENCE
What?

GRAVES *marches back along the corridor to try another room. His pretence of care for* CREDENCE *all but forgotten.*

GRAVES
You have magical ancestry,
but no power.

CREDENCE
But you said you could teach
me—

GRAVES
You're unteachable. Your
mother's dead. That's your
reward.

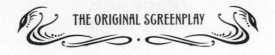

GRAVES *points to another landing.*

GRAVES
I'm done with you.

CREDENCE *doesn't move. He stares after* GRAVES, *his breathing becoming shallow and quick, as though he's trying to contain something.*

GRAVES *moves through the dark rooms. A tiny movement somewhere close.*

GRAVES
Modesty?

GRAVES *advances cautiously into a derelict schoolroom at the end of a corridor.*

SCENE 97
INT. TENEMENT IN THE BRONX, DERELICT ROOM—NIGHT

ANGLE ON MODESTY *cowering in a corner, wide-eyed with fear and shaking as* GRAVES *approaches.*

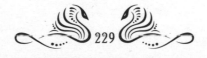

GRAVES
(whispering)
Modesty.

GRAVES *bends down and puts his wand away – once again playing the soothing parent.*

GRAVES
(gentle)
There's no need to be afraid.
I'm here with your brother,
Credence.

MODESTY *whimpers with terror at the mention of* CREDENCE.

GRAVES
Out you come now …

GRAVES *extends his hand.*

A faint jingle sounds.

ANGLE ON the ceiling as cracks begin to appear, spreading like a spider's web. Dust begins to fall as the walls shake uncontrollably, the room beginning to disintegrate around them.

GRAVES *stands. He looks down at* MODESTY, *but she is clearly terrified and not the source of this magic.* GRAVES *turns and slowly draws his wand, the wall in front of him collapsing as though turned to sand, revealing another wall ahead.* MODESTY *is nothing to him now.*

As each wall collapses in front of him he is transfixed, elated, yet also aware that he has made a colossal error ...

The final wall collapses. He is facing CREDENCE, *who stares at him, unable to control his fury, his sense of betrayal, his bitterness.*

GRAVES
Credence ... I owe you an apology ...

CREDENCE
I trusted you. I thought you were my friend. That you were different.

CREDENCE'S *face begins to contort, his rage tearing him from within.*

GRAVES
You can control it, Credence.

CREDENCE
(whispers, making eye contact finally)
But I don't think I want to, Mr Graves.

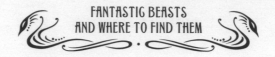

The Obscurus moves horribly beneath CREDENCE'S *skin. An awful inhuman growl comes out of his mouth, from which something dark begins to bloom.*

This force finally takes over CREDENCE, *his whole body exploding into a dark mass which hurtles forwards out of the window, narrowly missing* GRAVES.

GRAVES *stands, watching as the Obscurus zooms out and over the city.*

<u>SCENE 98</u>
EXT. TENEMENT IN THE BRONX—NIGHT

We follow the Obscurus as it churns and twists through the city, wreaking havoc: cars are sent flying, pavements explode and buildings are demolished – the Obscurus leaves only destruction in its wake.

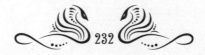

<u>SCENE 99</u>
EXT. SQUIRE'S ROOFTOP—NIGHT

NEWT, TINA, JACOB *and* QUEENIE *stand on the rooftop underneath a large 'SQUIRE'S' sign. From the edge they have a clear view of the chaos going on below.*

JACOB
(overstimulated)
Jeez ... is that the Obscuria-thing?

Sirens sound. NEWT *is staring, registering the scale of the destruction.*

NEWT
That's more powerful than any Obscurial I have ever heard of ...

A particularly loud explosion in the distance. The city beneath them is starting to burn. NEWT *thrusts his case into* TINA'S *hands and takes a journal from his pocket.*

NEWT
If I don't come back, look after my creatures. Everything that you need to know is in there.

He hands her the journal, barely able to make eye contact.

TINA

What?

NEWT

(looking back to the Obscurus)

They're not killing it.

Their eyes meet – a moment full of what they might have said to each other – before NEWT *jumps from the roof and Disapparates.*

TINA

(distraught)

NEWT!

TINA *slams the case into* QUEENIE'S *arms.*

TINA

You heard him – look after them!

TINA *also Disapparates.* QUEENIE *shoves the case at* JACOB.

QUEENIE

Keep holda that, honey.

She moves to Disapparate, but JACOB *hangs on to her and she falters.*

JACOB
No, no, no!

QUEENIE
I can't take you. Please let go of me, Jacob!

JACOB
Hey, hey! You're the one that said I was one of youse … right?

QUEENIE
It's too dangerous.

A further massive explosion in the distance. JACOB *tightens his grip on* QUEENIE. *She reads his mind and her expression changes to one of wonderment and tenderness as she sees what he went through in the war.* QUEENIE *is moved and appalled. Very slowly, she raises a hand and touches his cheek.*

SCENE 100
EXT. TIMES SQUARE—NIGHT

The scene is one of total chaos. Buildings are on fire, people scream and run in all directions, cars lie destroyed in the road.

GRAVES *prowls through the Square, oblivious to the distress around him, his focus concentrated on only one thing.*

The Obscurus writhes at one end of the Square, its energy angrier now – moving through layers of hurt and anguish, the products of isolation and torment – flecks of red light roaring from within. CREDENCE'S *face is just discernible*

within the mass, distorted, pained. GRAVES *stands before it, triumphant.*

NEWT *Apparates from further down the street and watches.*

GRAVES
(shouting to reach CREDENCE *over the almighty noise)*
To survive so long, with this inside you Credence, is a miracle. You are a miracle. Come with me – think of what we could achieve together.

The Obscurus moves closer to GRAVES *– we hear a scream from within the mass as its Dark energy bursts out once more, knocking* GRAVES *to the ground. The force sends a shockwave round the Square –* NEWT *dives behind a fallen car for cover.*

TINA *Apparates into the Square and takes cover by another burning vehicle close to* NEWT. *They look at each other.*

TINA
Newt!

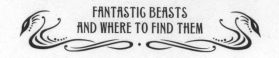

NEWT
It's the Second Salem boy.
He's the Obscurial.

TINA
He's not a child.

NEWT
I know – but I saw him – his power must be so strong – he's somehow managed to survive.

As the Obscurus screams once more, TINA *makes a decision.*

TINA
Newt! Save him.

TINA *dashes out towards* GRAVES. NEWT, *understanding, Disapparates.*

<u>SCENE 101</u>
EXT. TIMES SQUARE—NIGHT

GRAVES *is moving nearer and nearer to the Obscurus,*

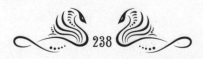

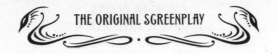

which continues to scream and wail at his presence. He takes out his wand, poised . . .

TINA *runs into view behind* GRAVES. *She fires at him, but he turns just in time – his reactions marvellous, astounding.*

The Obscurus now vanishes. GRAVES, *thoroughly irritated, advances on* TINA, *deflecting her spells with perfect ease.*

GRAVES

Tina. You're always turning up where you are least wanted.

GRAVES *summons an abandoned car, which whooshes through the air, forcing* TINA *to dive out of the way, just in time.*

By the time TINA *has gathered herself up from the ground,* GRAVES *has Disapparated.*

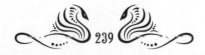

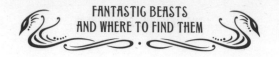

SCENE 102
INT. MAJOR INVESTIGATION DEPARTMENT, MACUSA—NIGHT

A metallic map of New York City lights up to show areas of intense magical activity. MADAM PICQUERY, *surrounded by top Aurors, looks on, aghast.*

MADAM PICQUERY
Contain this, or we are exposed and it will mean war.

The Aurors immediately Disapparate.

SCENE 103
EXT. ROOFTOPS OF NEW YORK—NIGHT

NEWT *race–Apparates as fast as he can across the tops of buildings in pursuit of the Obscurus.*

NEWT
Credence! Credence! I can help you.

The Obscurus dives towards NEWT, *who Disapparates just in time, before continuing to chase it across the rooftops.*

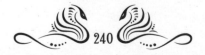

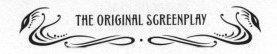

As he runs, spells explode around him, disintegrating the rooftops. A dozen Aurors have appeared, attacking the Obscurus from ahead, and almost taking out NEWT, *who leaps for cover, trying desperately to keep up.*

The Obscurus veers to avoid the spells, leaving black snow-like particles that drift across the rooftops as it retreats screaming, and turns down another block.

In a particularly vigorous display, the Obscurus now rises dramatically up into the air, as spells in electric blue and white hit it from all angles. Finally it crashes to the ground and races along a wide, empty street – a black tsunami destroying anything in its path.

<u>SCENE 104</u>
EXT. OUTSIDE A SUBWAY STATION—NIGHT

A line of policemen stand with their guns aimed at the terrifying supernatural force powering towards them.

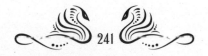

Their faces turn from confused alarm to total panic as they see the mass swarming ahead, making straight for them. They fire their guns – their efforts futile in the face of such a seemingly unstoppable kinetic mass. Finally

they disband, fleeing down the street, just as the Obscurus reaches them.

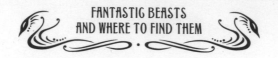

<u>SCENE 105</u>
EXT. ROOFTOPS/STREETS OF NEW YORK—NIGHT

ANGLE ON NEWT*, standing on top of a skyscraper looking out as the Obscurus rises up over the surrounding buildings and slams spectacularly into the ground just outside the City Hall subway entrance.*

Sudden quiet. A pulsing, heaving, screechy breathing emanates from the Obscurus where it rests at the entrance.

Finally, as NEWT *watches, we see the black mass shrink to nothing, and the small figure of* CREDENCE *descends the steps into the subway.*

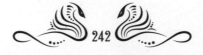

SCENE 106
INT. SUBWAY—NIGHT

NEWT *Apparates into the City Hall subway, a long, mosaiced Art Deco station tunnel, which bears the signs of having been crossed by the Obscurus: the chandelier creaks, a few tiles have fallen. We can hear its deep breathing, cornered, like a frightened panther.*

NEWT *creeps along the platform, trying to find the epicentre of the sound, as the Obscurus slides down the ceiling.*

<u>SCENE 107</u>
EXT. SUBWAY ENTRANCE—NIGHT

Aurors surround the entrance to the subway. Pointing their wands at the pavement and into the sky, they draw an invisible energy field around the entrance.

We hear more Aurors arrive, among them GRAVES *– scanning, calculating and immediately taking charge.*

GRAVES
Bar the area. I don't want anyone else down there!

As the magical field is almost complete, a figure rolls underneath it and dashes unseen into the subway – TINA.

<u>SCENE 108</u>
INT. SUBWAY—NIGHT

NEWT *has reached the Obscurus in the shadows of a tunnel. Now much calmer, it gently swirls in the air above the train tracks.* NEWT *hides behind a pillar as he talks.*

NEWT
Credence . . . it's Credence isn't it? I'm here to help you, Credence. I'm not here to hurt you.

In the distance we hear footsteps, the pacing controlled, deliberate.

NEWT *moves out from behind the pillar, and steps onto the train tracks. Within the mass of the Obscurus we can see a shadow of* CREDENCE*, curled up, scared.*

NEWT
I've met someone just like

you, Credence. A girl – a young girl who'd been imprisoned, she had been locked away and she'd been punished for her magic.

CREDENCE *is listening – he never dreamed there was another. Slowly the Obscurus melts away, leaving only* CREDENCE, *huddled on the train tracks – a frightened child.*

NEWT *crouches on the floor.* CREDENCE *looks to him, the tiniest trace of hope dawning in his expression: might there be a way back?*

NEWT

Credence, can I come over to you? Can I come over?

NEWT *slowly moves forwards, but as he does so a sharp burst of light blazes out from the darkness and a spell strikes, throwing him backwards.*

GRAVES *marches down the tunnel with intense purpose.*

CREDENCE *begins to run as* GRAVES *fires further spells at* NEWT, *who rolls out of the way towards the tunnel's central pillars. From here* NEWT *tries to fire back, but his efforts are easily deflected.*

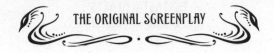

CREDENCE *continues to lumber down the tracks but stops – a rabbit caught in the headlights – as a train approaches, its lights glaring from the darkness.*

It is up to GRAVES *to save* CREDENCE *– magically casting him out of the train's path.*

<u>SCENE 109</u>
EXT. SUBWAY ENTRANCE—NIGHT

MADAM PICQUERY *surveys the situation from under the magical forcefield.*

ANGLE FROM the crowd and police's POV:

People begin to swarm around the subway, their cries and chatter becoming louder as they stare at the magical bubble surrounding the subway. Reporters have appeared, photographing the scene with an increased frenzy.

SHAW SR *and* BARKER *push their way through the crowd.*

SHAW SR
That thing killed my son – I want justice!

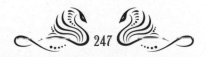

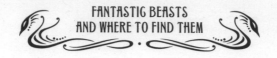

CLOSE ON MADAM PICQUERY *as she looks out to the crowd.*

SHAW SR (*O.S.*)
I'll expose you for who you are and what you've done.

SCENE 110
INT. SUBWAY—NIGHT

GRAVES *stands on the platform, continuing to duel with* NEWT, *who stands on the train tracks.* CREDENCE *cowers behind* NEWT.

Finally, almost bored by NEWT'S *efforts,* GRAVES *casts a spell that ripples along the train tracks and down the tunnel, finally blasting into* NEWT, *throwing him high into the air.*

NEWT *lands on his back and* GRAVES *immediately sets upon him, casting spells in a whip-like motion with increasing vigour.* GRAVES'S *immense power is evident, as* NEWT *writhes on the ground, unable to stop him.*

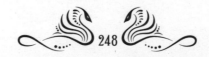

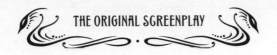

<u>SCENE 111</u>
EXT. SUBWAY ENTRANCE—NIGHT

WIDE SHOT:

We see the luminous wall of vibrating energy now flashing with the power of the magic it contains.

LANGDON, *drunk, stares, enthralled and amazed by the spectacle.*

SHAW SR
(to the photographers around him)
Look! Take photos!

<u>SCENE 112</u>
INT. SUBWAY—NIGHT

GRAVES *continues to whip* NEWT, *a manic, crazed look in his eyes.*

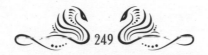

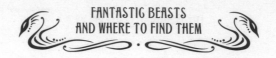

CLOSE ON CREDENCE, *further down the tunnel, sobbing. He begins to shake, his face slowly turning black as he tries to stop the kinetic mass from rising up within him.*

As NEWT *cries out in pain,* CREDENCE *succumbs to the blackness – his body enveloped and overcome – the Obscurus rising up and blasting down the tunnel towards* GRAVES.

GRAVES *is mesmerised – he falls to his knees beneath the vast black mass – pleading in wonder.*

GRAVES

Credence.

The Obscurus lets out an unearthly scream and dives towards GRAVES, *who Disapparates just in time. The Obscurus continues to blast around the tunnel.*

GRAVES *and* NEWT *Disapparate and Apparate around the subway trying to avoid the Obscurus's path. This causes the station to disintegrate even faster. Suddenly, the force accelerates, becoming a giant wave that consumes the entire space before flying out through the roof.*

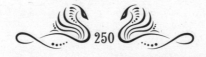

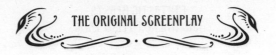

SCENE 113
EXT. SUBWAY ENTRANCE—NIGHT

The Obscurus crashes up through the pavement, watched by wizards and No-Majs alike. It storms up a half-built skyscraper, windows shattering at every level, electric wiring exploding, until it reaches the skeletal framework of scaffolding above, which buckles perilously.

Below it, the crowd outside the magical cordon runs for cover, terrified.

The Obscurus forms a wide disc shape before plunging back down into the subway.

SCENE 114
INT. SUBWAY—NIGHT

The Obscurus screams and dives, bursting through the subway roof – for a split second, both NEWT *and* GRAVES *seem on the point of death as they lie on the tracks, cowering beneath this Dark force.*

TINA *(O.S.)*
CREDENCE, NO!

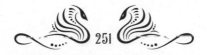

TINA *runs onto the tracks.*

Inches from GRAVES'S *face, the Obscurus freezes. Slowly, very slowly, it rises back up, swirling more gently, staring at* TINA, *who looks straight back into its weird eyes.*

TINA

Don't do this – please.

NEWT

Keep talking, Tina. Keep talking to him – he'll listen to you. He's listening.

Inside the Obscurus, CREDENCE *reaches out to* TINA, *the only person who has ever done him an uncomplicated kindness. He looks at her, desperate and afraid. He has dreamed of her ever since she saved him from a beating.*

TINA

I know what that woman did to you . . . I know that you've suffered . . . you need to stop this now . . . Newt and I will protect you . . .

GRAVES *is on his feet.*

TINA
(pointing to GRAVES*)*
This man – he is using you.

GRAVES
Don't listen to her, Credence. I want you to be free. It's all right.

TINA
(to CREDENCE*, calming him)*
That's it . . .

The Obscurus is beginning to shrink. Its dreadful face is becoming more human, more like CREDENCE'S *own.*

Suddenly Aurors begin pouring down the steps of the subway and into the tunnel. More Aurors advance from behind TINA*, their wands raised aggressively.*

TINA
Shhhh! Don't, you'll frighten him.

The Obscurus lets out a terrible moan and begins to swell again. The station is crumbling. NEWT *and* TINA *wheel around, arms akimbo, both trying to protect* CREDENCE.

GRAVES *spins to face the Aurors, wand at the ready.*

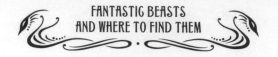

GRAVES
Wands down! Anyone harms him – they'll answer to me—
(turning back to CREDENCE*)*
Credence!

TINA
Credence . . .

The Aurors begin pelting the Obscurus with spells.

GRAVES
NO!

We see CREDENCE *from within the black mass, his face contorted, screaming. The tirade of spells continues and* CREDENCE *howls in pain.*

SCENE 115
EXT. SUBWAY ENTRANCE—NIGHT

The magical force field surrounding the subway breaks down as people continue to flee the scene. Only SHAW SR *and* LANGDON *stand steadfast.*

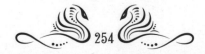

SCENE 116
INT. SUBWAY—NIGHT

Aurors continue to aim spells at the Obscurus, their efforts unrelenting and brutal.

Under this pressure, the Obscurus finally seems to implode – a white ball of magical light taking over from the black mass.

The force of the change sends TINA, NEWT *and the Aurors stumbling backwards.*

All power subsides. Only small tatters of black matter are left – floating through the air like feathers.

NEWT *gets to his feet, his face racked with deep-felt grief.* TINA *remains on the floor, crying.*

GRAVES, *however, climbs up, back onto the platform, as close as possible to the remnants of the black mass.*

The Aurors advance towards GRAVES.

GRAVES
You fools. Do you realise what you've done?

GRAVES *seethes as the others watch him with interest.* MADAM PICQUERY *emerges from behind the Aurors, her tone steely, questioning.*

MADAM PICQUERY
The Obscurial was killed on
my orders, Mr Graves.

GRAVES
Yes. And history will surely
note that, Madam President.

GRAVES *moves towards her along the platform, his tone threatening.*

GRAVES
What was done here tonight
was not right!

MADAM PICQUERY
He was responsible for
the death of a No-Maj. He
risked the exposure of our
community. He has broken
one of our most sacred laws.

GRAVES
(laughing bitterly)
A law that has us scuttling
like rats in the gutter! A
law that demands that we

conceal our true nature! A law that directs those under its dominion to cower in fear lest we risk discovery! I ask you Madam President—

(eyes flashing to all present)

—I ask all of you. Who does this law protect? Us?

(gesturing vaguely to the No-Majs above)

Or them?

(smiling bitterly)

I refuse to bow down any longer.

GRAVES *walks away from the Aurors.*

MADAM PICQUERY

(to the Aurors flanking her)

Aurors, I'd like you to relieve Mr Graves of his wand and escort him back to—

As GRAVES *moves down the platform a wall of white light suddenly appears in front of him, blocking his path.*

GRAVES *thinks for a moment – a sneer of derision and irritation crossing his face. He turns.*

GRAVES *strides confidently back along the platform, firing spells at both groups of Aurors facing him. Spells fly back at him from all angles, but* GRAVES *parries them all. Several Aurors are sent flying –* GRAVES *appears to be winning . . .*

In a split-second NEWT *pulls the cocoon from his pocket and releases it at* GRAVES. *The Swooping Evil soars around him, shielding* NEWT *and the Aurors from* GRAVES'S *spells, and giving* NEWT *time to raise his wand.*

With a sense that he's been holding this one back, he slashes it through the air: out flies a crackling rope of supernatural light that wraps itself around GRAVES *like a whip.* GRAVES *tries to hold it off as it tightens but staggers, struggles and falls to his knees, dropping his wand.*

TINA

Accio.

GRAVES'S *wand flies into* TINA'S *hand.* GRAVES *looks around at them, a deep hatred in his eyes.*

NEWT *and* TINA *slowly advance,* NEWT *raising his wand.*

NEWT

Revelio.

GRAVES *transforms. He is no longer dark, but blond and blue-eyed. He is the man on the posters. A murmur spreads through the crowd: GRINDELWALD.*

MADAM PICQUERY *moves towards him.*

GRINDELWALD
(with contempt)
Do you think *you* can hold *me?*

MADAM PICQUERY
We'll do our best, Mr Grindelwald.

GRINDELWALD *stares intently at* MADAM PICQUERY, *his expression of disgust turning into a small, derisory smile. He is forced to his feet by two Aurors, who move him towards the entrance.*

As GRINDELWALD *reaches* NEWT, *he pauses – both smiling and sneering.*

GRINDELWALD
Will we die, just a little?

He is led away up and out of the subway. NEWT *watches, bemused.*

TIME CUT:

QUEENIE *and* JACOB *push their way through to the front of the Aurors.* JACOB *holds* NEWT'S *case.*

QUEENIE *hugs* TINA. NEWT *stares at* JACOB.

JACOB
Hey . . . I figured somebody oughta keep an eye on this thing.

He hands NEWT *his case.*

NEWT
(humble, completely grateful)
Thank you.

MADAM PICQUERY *addresses the group as she stares through the broken roof of the subway station, into the world outside.*

MADAM PICQUERY
We owe you an apology, Mr Scamander. But the magical community is exposed! We cannot Obliviate an entire city.

A beat as this sinks in.

As NEWT *follows* MADAM PICQUERY'S *gaze, he sees a tendril of black matter, a small part of the Obscurus, floating down through the roof. Unnoticed by anyone else, it eventually floats up and away, trying to reconnect with its host.*

A pause. NEWT'S *attention snaps back to the problem at hand.*

NEWT
Actually, I think we can.

TIME CUT:

NEWT *has placed his case wide open underneath the huge hole in the subway roof.*

PUSH IN CLOSE ON NEWT'S *open case.*

Suddenly FRANK *bursts forth in a flurry of feathers and gushes of wind – the crowd of Aurors backs away. The creature is beautiful, mesmerising but scary as he flaps his powerful wings and hovers above them.*

NEWT *moves forward – he examines* FRANK, *a look of real tenderness and pride on his face.*

NEWT
I was intending to wait until
we got to Arizona, but it
seems like now you are our
only hope, Frank.

A look between them – an understanding. NEWT *reaches*

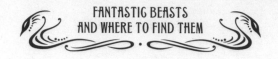

out his arm and FRANK *presses his beak lovingly into the embrace – they nuzzle each other affectionately.*

The assembled group watches in awe.

NEWT
I'll miss you, too.

NEWT *steps back, taking the flask of Swooping Evil venom from his pocket.*

NEWT
(*to* FRANK)
You know what you've got to do.

NEWT *throws the vial high up into the air –* FRANK *lets out a sharp cry, catching it in his beak and immediately soaring out of the subway.*

SCENE 117
EXT. NEW YORK—SKY—DAWN

No-Majs and Aurors alike shriek and recoil as FRANK *bursts forth from the subway, gliding into the dawn-lit sky.*

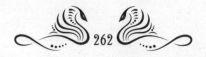

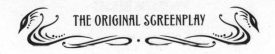

We follow FRANK *as he rises higher and higher into the air. As his wings flap harder, faster, storm clouds congregate. Lightning flashes. We spiral upwards as* FRANK *twists and turns, leaving New York lying far below.*

CLOSE ON FRANK'S *beak, the vial clutched tightly and finally crushed. The powerful venom spreads through the thick rain, enchanting it, thickening it. The darkening sky flashes a brilliant blue and rain begins to fall.*

SCENE 118
EXT. SUBWAY ENTRANCE—DAWN

HIGH ANGLE pushing down towards the crowd as they look up to the sky. As the rain falls and hits them, people move on, docile – their bad memories washed away. Each person goes about their daily business as though nothing unusual has happened.

Aurors move through the streets, performing repairing charms to rebuild the city: buildings and cars are reconstructed and streets are returned to normal.

ANGLE ON LANGDON, *standing in the rain, his expression softening, growing blank as the water runs over his face.*

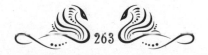

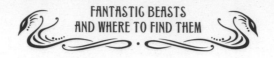

ANGLE ON police looking at their guns, confused – why do they have them drawn? They slowly gather themselves, putting their weapons away.

Inside a small family home, a young mother looks on fondly at her family. As she takes a sip of water, her expression becomes blank.

Groups of Aurors continue to repair the streets, swiftly reassembling broken tram tracks, all traces of destruction finally disappearing. One Auror, passing a newsstand, enchants the papers, removing NEWT *and* TINA'S *mugshots and replacing them with banal headlines about the weather.*

MR BINGLEY, *the bank manager, stands in his bathroom taking a shower. As the water trickles over him, he too is Obliviated. We see* BINGLEY'S *wife, brushing her teeth, her expression vacant, carefree.*

FRANK *continues to soar through the streets of New York, churning up more and more rain as he goes, his feathers shimmering a brilliant gold. Finally he glides into the breaking New York dawn, a magnificent sight.*

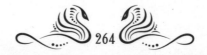

<u>SCENE 119</u>
INT. SUBWAY PLATFORM—DAWN

As MADAM PICQUERY *looks on, the roof of the subway is swiftly repaired.*

NEWT *addresses the group.*

NEWT
They won't remember anything. That venom has incredibly powerful Obliviative properties.

MADAM PICQUERY
(impressed)
We owe you a great debt, Mr Scamander. Now – get that case out of New York.

NEWT
Yes, Madam President.

MADAM PICQUERY *begins to walk away, her pack of Aurors moving with her. Suddenly she turns back.* QUEENIE, *having read her mind, stands protectively in front of* JACOB, *trying to hide him.*

MADAM PICQUERY
Is that No-Maj still here?

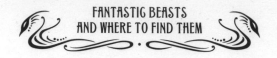

(*on seeing* JACOB)
Obliviate him. There can be no exceptions.

MADAM PICQUERY *reads the anguish in their faces.*

MADAM PICQUERY
I'm sorry – but even one witness . . . you know the law.

A pause. She is uncomfortable at their distress.

MADAM PICQUERY
I'll let you say goodbye.

She leaves.

SCENE 120
EXT. SUBWAY—DAWN

JACOB *leads the others up the steps of the subway,* QUEENIE *following close behind him.*

Rain is still falling heavily, the streets now almost empty but for a few hard-working Aurors.

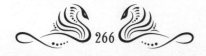

JACOB *has reached the top of the steps and stands, gazing into the rain.* QUEENIE *reaches out and grabs his coat, willing him not to move out into the street.* JACOB *turns to her.*

JACOB
Hey. Hey this is for the best.
(off their looks)
Yeah – I was – I was never
even supposed to be here.

JACOB *fights back tears.* QUEENIE *gazes up at him, her beautiful face full of distress.* TINA *and* NEWT, *too, look incredibly sad.*

JACOB
I was never supposed to
know any of this. Everybody
knows Newt only kept me
around because – hey –
Newt, why did you keep me
around?

NEWT *has to be explicit. It doesn't come easily.*

NEWT
Because I like you. Because
you're my friend and I'll
never forget how you helped
me, Jacob.

A beat. JACOB *is overcome with emotion at* NEWT'S *answer.*

JACOB

Oh!

QUEENIE *moves forwards up the stairs towards* JACOB – *they stand close.*

QUEENIE

(trying to cheer him up)

I'll come with you. We'll go somewhere – we'll go anywhere – see I ain't never gonna find anyone like—

JACOB

(bravely)

There's loads like me.

QUEENIE

No ... no ... there's only one like you.

The pain is almost unbearable.

JACOB

(a beat)

I gotta go.

JACOB *turns to face the rain, and wipes his eyes.*

NEWT
(starting after him)
JACOB!

JACOB
(trying to smile)
It's okay … it's okay … it's okay. It's just like waking up, right?

The group smiles back at him, encouraging, trying to soothe the situation.

Looking at their faces as he moves, JACOB *walks backwards into the rain. Turning his face to the sky, arms out, he allows the water to wash over him completely.*

QUEENIE *creates a magical umbrella with her wand and steps out towards* JACOB. *She moves in closely, tenderly stroking* JACOB'S *face before closing her eyes and bending in to gently kiss him.*

Finally she pulls slowly away, her gaze not leaving JACOB'S *face even for a second. Then, suddenly, she's gone, leaving* JACOB *standing, arms out, longingly embracing no one.*

CLOSE ON JACOB'S *face as he fully 'wakes up', blank-faced and confused by his location and the torrential downpour he's standing in. He finally moves off through the streets – a lonely figure.*

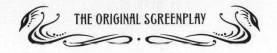

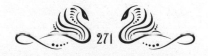

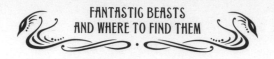

SCENE 121

EXT. JACOB'S CANNING FACTORY—A WEEK LATER—EARLY EVENING

An exhausted JACOB*, surrounded by a crowd of similarly overalled production-line workers, is leaving after a hard day's shift. He carries a battered leather case.*

A man walks towards him – NEWT*. They collide and* JACOB'S *case is knocked to the ground.*

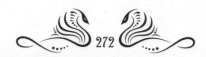

NEWT
So sorry – sorry!

NEWT *has moved swiftly and purposefully onwards.*

JACOB
(no recognition)
Hey!

JACOB *bends to pick up his case and looks down, puzzled. His old case is suddenly very heavy. One of the catches flicks open of its own accord.* JACOB *smiles a little, and bends down to open the case.*

Inside, the case is filled with solid silver Occamy eggshells, a note attached. As JACOB *reads, we hear:*

NEWT (*V.O.*)
'Dear Mr Kowalski, You are wasted in a canning factory. Please take these Occamy eggshells as collateral for your bakery. A well-wisher.'

<u>SCENE 122</u>
EXT. NEW YORK HARBOUR—NEXT DAY

CLOSE ON NEWT'S *feet as he walks through the crowd.*

NEWT *is preparing to leave New York, overcoat on, Hufflepuff scarf around his neck, case tied up tightly with string.*

TINA *walks alongside him. They stop before the boarding gate.* TINA *looks anxious.*

NEWT
(smiling)
Well it's been . . .

TINA
Hasn't it!

Pause. NEWT *looks up,* TINA'S *expression is expectant.*

TINA
Listen, Newt, I wanted to thank you.

NEWT
What on earth for?

TINA
Well, you know, if you hadn't said all those nice things to Madam Picquery about me – I wouldn't be back on the investigative team now.

NEWT
Well – I can't think of anyone that I'd rather have investigating me.

Not precisely what he was aiming for, but too late now . . . NEWT *becomes slightly awkward,* TINA *shyly appreciative.*

TINA

Well try not to need investigating for a bit.

NEWT

I will. Quiet life for me from now on ... back to the Ministry ... deliver my manuscript ...

TINA

I'll look out for it. *Fantastic Beasts and Where to Find Them.*

Weak smiles. A pause. TINA *plucks up courage.*

TINA

Does Leta Lestrange like to read?

NEWT

Who?

TINA

The girl whose picture you carry—

NEWT

I don't really know what Leta likes these days because people change.

TINA

Yes.

NEWT

(a dawning realisation)

I've changed. I think. Maybe a little.

TINA *is delighted, but doesn't know how to express it. Instead, she's trying not to cry. The ship's siren sounds – most of the other passengers have now boarded.*

NEWT

I'll send you a copy of my book, if I may.

TINA

I'd like that.

NEWT *gazes at* TINA *– awkwardly affectionate. He gently reaches forward and touches her hair. Lingering for a moment, they stare into each other's eyes.*

A last look and NEWT *suddenly moves away, leaving* TINA *standing, raising a hand to touch where* NEWT *stroked her hair.*

But then he's back.

NEWT
I'm so sorry – how would you feel if I gave you your copy in person?

A radiant smile breaks across TINA'S *face.*

TINA
I'd like that – very much.

NEWT *can't help but grin back at her before turning and walking away.*

He pauses on the gangplank, perhaps unsure of how to act, but eventually moves on without looking back.

TINA *stands alone in the empty harbour. As she walks away, there's a playful skip to her step.*

SCENE 123

EXT. JACOB'S BAKERY, LOWER EAST SIDE—THREE MONTHS LATER—DAY

WIDE SHOT of a bustling New York street – market stalls line the street, which heaves with busy people, horses and carriages.

ANGLE ON a small, inviting bakery. Crowds throng outside the pretty little shop, painted with the name 'KOWALSKI'. People peer with interest into the shop's windows, and happy customers leave, their arms laden with baked goods.

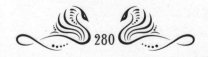

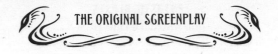

SCENE 124

INT. JACOB'S BAKERY, LOWER EAST SIDE—DAY

CLOSE ON the doorbell as it rings to signal the entrance of a new customer.

CLOSE ON the pastries and breads on the counter, all moulded into fanciful little shapes – we recognise the Demiguise, Niffler and Erumpent among them.

JACOB, *serving, is very happy, his shop full to bursting with customers.*

FEMALE CUSTOMER
(examining the little pastries)
Where do you get your ideas from, Mr Kowalski?

JACOB
I don't know, I don't know – they just come!

He hands the lady her pastries.

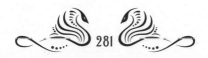

JACOB
Here you go – don't forget this – enjoy.

JACOB *turns and calls over one of his bakery assistants, handing him a pair of keys.*

JACOB
Hey, Henry – storage, all right? Thanks, pal.

The bell tinkles again.

JACOB *looks up and is thunderstruck all over again: it's* QUEENIE. *They stare at each other* – QUEENIE *beams, radiant.* JACOB, *quizzical and totally enchanted, touches his neck – a flicker of memory. He smiles back.*

THE

END

ACKNOWLEDGEMENTS

Without the patience and wisdom of Steve Kloves and David Yates, there would be no Fantastic Beasts screenplay. They have my boundless gratitude for every note, every piece of encouragement, every improvement they suggested. Learning, in Steve's immortal words, to 'fit the woman to the dress' has been a fascinating, challenging, exasperating, exhilarating, infuriating and ultimately rewarding experience that I wouldn't have missed for the world. I couldn't have done it without them.

David Heyman has been with me from the very first step of Harry Potter's transition to the big screen, and Fantastic Beasts would have been immeasurably poorer without him. It's been a very long journey since that first queasy lunch in Soho, and he is currently bringing to Newt all the knowledge, dedication and expertise that he brought to Harry Potter.

There would never have been a Fantastic Beasts franchise without Kevin Tsujihara. Even though I've been carrying the germ of the idea for Fantastic Beasts since 2001, when I wrote the initial book for charity, it took Kevin to make me commit to bringing Newt's story to the big screen. His support

has been invaluable and he deserves the lion's share of the credit for making this happen.

Last, but never least, my family have been enormously supportive of this project even though it has meant me working through a year's worth of vacations. I don't know where I'd be without you, except that it would be a dark and lonely place where I wouldn't feel like inventing anything. So, to Neil, Jessica, David and Kenzie: thank you for being completely wonderful, funny and loving, and for still believing that I should pursue Fantastic Beasts, however tricky and time-consuming they may sometimes be.

GLOSSARY OF FILM TERMS

Back to scene: After focusing on one character or action within a scene, the camera returns to the larger scene.

Close on: The camera films a person or object from close range.

Ext.: Exterior; an outside location.

Flashcut: An extremely brief transition shot, sometimes as short as one frame.

High wide: The camera is placed above, 'looking down' on the subject or scene from a wide angle.

Hold on: The camera rests on a person or object.

Int.: Interior; an indoor location.

Jump cut: Cutting from one important moment to the next from the same angle. This transition is usually used to show a very brief time lapse.

Montage: A series of shots in a sequence condensing space, time and information, often with music accompanying it.

O.S.: *Off-screen*; action that takes place off-screen or dialogue that is spoken without the character being shown on screen.

Pan/whip pan: Camera movement involving the camera turning on a stationary axis moving slowly from one subject to another; whip pan is a very fast move from one subject to the other.

POV: *Point-of-view*; the camera films from a particular character's point of view.

***Sotto voce*:** Spoken at a whisper or under one's breath.

Time cut: Cutting to later in the same scene.

V.O.: *Voice-over*; dialogue spoken by a character not present in the scene on screen.

Wide shot: The camera shows the entire object or human figure, usually to place it in relation to its surroundings. It is often used to set the scene in a film.

Warner Bros. Pictures Presents
a Heyday Films Production
a David Yates Film

FANTASTIC BEASTS AND WHERE TO FIND THEM

Directed by . . . . David Yates

Written by . . . . J.K. Rowling

Produced by . . . . David Heyman p.g.a., J.K. Rowling p.g.a., Steve Kloves p.g.a., Lionel Wigram p.g.a.

Executive Producers . . . . Tim Lewis, Neil Blair, Rick Senat

Director of Photography . . . . Philippe Rousselot, A.F.C./ASC

Production Designer . . . . Stuart Craig

Editor . . . . Mark Day

Costume Designer . . . . Colleen Atwood

Music . . . . James Newton Howard

STARRING

NEWT SCAMANDER . . . . Eddie Redmayne
TINA GOLDSTEIN . . . . Katherine Waterston
JACOB KOWALSKI . . . . Dan Fogler
QUEENIE GOLDSTEIN . . . . Alison Sudol
CREDENCE BAREBONE . . . . Ezra Miller
MARY LOU BAREBONE . . . . Samantha Morton
HENRY SHAW SR . . . . Jon Voight
SERAPHINA PICQUERY . . . . Carmen Ejogo

and

PERCIVAL GRAVES . . . . Colin Farrell

ABOUT THE AUTHOR

J.K. Rowling is the author of the bestselling Harry Potter series of seven books, published between 1997 and 2007, which have sold over 450 million copies worldwide, are distributed in more than 200 territories and translated into 79 languages, and have been turned into eight blockbuster films by Warner Bros. She has written three companion volumes to the series in aid of charity: *Quidditch Through the Ages* and *Fantastic Beasts and Where to Find Them* in aid of Comic Relief; and *The Tales of Beedle the Bard* in aid of her children's charity, Lumos. Her website and e-publisher Pottermore is the digital hub of the Wizarding World. She collaborated with writer Jack Thorne and director John Tiffany on the stage play *Harry Potter and the Cursed Child Parts One and Two,* which premiered in 2016 in London's West End. J.K. Rowling is also the author of a novel for adult readers, *The Casual Vacancy,* and, under the pseudonym Robert Galbraith, of three crime novels featuring private detective Cormoran Strike, which are to be adapted for BBC television. *Fantastic Beasts and Where to Find Them* is J.K. Rowling's first screenplay.

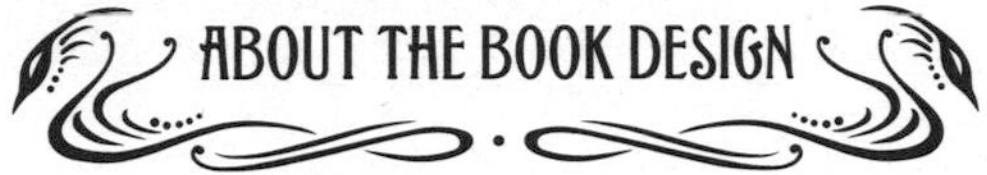

ABOUT THE BOOK DESIGN

This book was designed by MinaLima, an award-winning design studio founded by Miraphora Mina and Eduardo Lima, who were graphic designers on *Fantastic Beasts and Where to Find Them* and on the eight Harry Potter films.

The cover and illustrations in this book were based on creatures in the story and inspired by 1920s decorative style. They were drawn by hand and finished digitally in Adobe Illustrator.

The text was set in Crimson Text and the display type was set in Sheridan Gothic SG.